THE SEEKERS

THE DRAGON

DENISE W. MCGRAIN

Printed in the United States of America

Library of Congress Control Number: 2018934829
eBook: 978-1-948172-17-2
Softcover: 978-1-948172-05-9

STONEWALL PRESS
PAVING YOUR WAY TO SUCCESS

Stonewall Press
363 Paladium Court
Owings Mills, MD 21117
www.stonewallpress.com
1-888-334-0980

PROLOGUE

The winter was long and cold as the Confederate Army trudged into Dalton. General Joseph E. Johnston and his men were tired and hungry after their defeat in Chattanooga. Johnston received word that Major General William Sherman was leading his troops in a mission to invade Atlanta. By this time, Johnston's men had faced many tragedies. He worried that this would break what little spirit they had left. He would need more time to allow them to recover. Johnson knew his men would be in danger of running into Union soldiers if he chose to take the path through the small towns, so he decided to entrench his men in Dalton along the Rocky Face Ridge on the outskirts of town.

During the next six months, Johnston joined forces with Major General Polk. This merger made their army 70,000-men strong and gave the troops new confidence. That was exactly what Johnston hoped for, although he, along with the other commanding officers, knew it held little hope against Sherman's 110,000.

The first skirmish hit the Confederate Calvary at Tunnel Hill and fought through to Rocky Face Ridge. For the next two days, Sherman's men attacked against Johnston's forces in several small-scale attacks. But the Confederates stood strong and held their position. The ambushes were merely a diversion. In the meantime, Sherman had gathered his commanders around to discuss a new plan. "Men, right now the Confederated Army is too well entrenched, but knowing Johnston, his attention will be so focused on the Union Army out there in front he won't even take into account what's going on behind the lines, so I have devised a new strategy."

By early Sunday morning, Sherman's plan had been carried out. The fighting at Resaca was in full force and, by that afternoon, celebrations started early among the Union soldiers as they helped themselves to their first round of drinks. Before long, things grew out of control. Some Union soldiers began looting and pillaging the small town; what men weren't killed during the raids fled on foot to their homes to gather their families and secure a way out.

One of Sherman's men broke down the door of a shop where a shopkeeper's family lived. He stood at the back of the shop scanning the hallway until he spotted the shopkeeper standing in the dark at the back of the house. Squinting his eyes, he slowly raised his gun and shot him in the chest. The shopkeeper's wife heard a shot coming from the hall. As she closed the pantry door, she pressed her finger against her lips then pushed her daughter in deeper. She motioned for her to stay put and silent while she exited the pantry, then slammed the door to create a commotion as she ran down the hallway. The sound of her footsteps distracted the soldier as she passed him. He reached out and grabbed at her arm, but she jerked away and darted for the front door. He tried again and, this time, got her. He felt for his knife with his free hand and cut her throat. She dropped to the floor and blood gushed from her throat. The young daughter could hear her mother gurgling from the other room as she suffocated. When the room grew quiet, the terrified daughter stared through a crack in the door and watched the soldier kick her mother's body out of the way as he walked into the kitchen, past the table into the sitting room. A strange light flashed behind him. Although startled by the light display, she was too overwhelmed by grief to give it much thought. She then moved by pure instinct, running quickly out the backdoor to a cluster of trees that lined the town's main road. The rain was coming in relentless drizzles. As she ran, her arms and face scraped against the branches. She slipped and fell on the wet ground. Getting up, she brushed her hair away and wiped the water from her eyes. After going a short way, her shoe caught on a root and she fell again against the base of a large oak tree. Suddenly hearing voices, the terrified girl hid behind the old tree and tried to bury herself underneath the dead branches. One of the Union soldiers heard shuffling noises not far from the campsite. Drunk, he stumbled over to see what was scratching around in the woods. He circled the tree until he found a pair of large blue eyes peeking out at him from beneath soaked hair that clung to the sides of her face. She squeezed closer against the base of the tree while he started laughing.

"Come on out, sweetheart. Let's have a look at ya!" His slurred words made the young girl press harder against the tree.

"What's wrong, girl?"

As he breathed out, she inhaled his strong, foul breath heavy with the smell of whiskey. The unpleasant odor poured over her as he reached down to grab her arm and lift her away from the tree. He jerked harder, butshe refused to move; her eyes not shifting from the gun in his other hand now pointing at her! Pulling once again, he yanked her to her feet just as his gun went off and shot through her! The soldier looked down at his gun, as if noticing it for the first time, and then back at the girl. He watched the blood gushed from her left side. Panicked, he knew what this would cost him! Quickly, he set to work as he shoved and stuffed the young girl's body back down against the side of the tree and scraped around to cover her body with the dead leaves piled in a small heap on the ground. When he finished, he stood still for a moment, looking down at the small mound, waiting, listening to see if she might stir or make a noise.

The young girl lay still, hoping he would leave. Finally, the soldier turned and left. *She's dead, the body's not moving*, he thought to himself.

Fighting to keep from struggling and trying not to scream out in pain, she bit down hard on her lips. Her breath trickled out of her as now, she's filled with relief that the solider walked away. She was safe, the heaviness was gone! The trees and grass were fading, the townspeople's blood; she couldn't see it anymore running along the ground. There were no more cries for mercy, no loud shots from the battlefield on the other side of the hill, everything was silent as she slipped quietly away into darkness.

CHAPTER ONE

"Is she breathing?"

Voices…sounds like voices…whispering, what are they? Never mind, it's warm and comfortable in here, I just want to sleep a little more… don't want to be bothered.

"Her pulse is low, but her levels are improving. Her skin is getting warmer. Wipe away the dirt from her face and neck. It looks like we're going to have to cut her clothes away from her body," the voices said.

She felt fingers sliding along her jawline down to the side of her throat. She felt a cold hardness gliding along her sides, then air whispered across her skin as something fell away from her arms and legs.

"The pulse in her throat is getting stronger. Just give her a few more minutes and then we'll wake her up."

Lifting her eyelashes just a little, she peeked through her eyelids. *So bright! Have I died and gone to heaven?* Looking closer, she saw shadows moving around. *Were those angels?* Flashes brighten the room. She squeezed her eyelids closed again.

"Miss, can you open your eyes?" a voice said.

She felt someone nudging her arm.

"Miss, open your eyes now. We need you to respond."

Blinking, she looked around at everyone in the room, shielding her eyes through her lashes. A man was bending toward her, closely watching her. He didn't look too old, maybe thirty-five or forty. His hair was blond and he had a small beard on his face. The only clothes he seemed to be wearing was a white coat. *It looks like he's pulling on his skin, maybe stretching it, but it's probably gloves, but yuck! It looks gross. I've never seen clear colored gloves before!* He let go of the glove, making a popping noise, flexing his fingers as he bent closer again. She squeezed her eyes shut.

"Miss… don't be afraid. I know this is difficult for you, but look… let's start with something easy. Tell me little something about yourself."

Peeking through her eyelashes again, she looked straight into a pair of pale blue eyes. *He's trying to make me feel better, but it's not helping. This room is really strange.*

"Okay, I'll go first, I'm a doctor, Dr. Ben Jacob. I know you are… Melissa Fuller. Can you tell me anything else about yourself?"

What!? How' d he found out my name? Who are these people? Where am I?

He reached out to help her sit up, but she shrank away from him. He slowly stepped back holding both of his hands up, palms out.

"Alright, Melissa, you can get up on your own. Be careful, you've been injured. We had to put a few stitches in, so take it easy," said Dr. Jacob.

At his words, she felt pain in her left side, her hand automatically went to the injury. Her eyes opened all the way at the feel of the stitches. Memories of hiding in the food pantry while watching her father being murdered and her mother motioning for her to stay hidden came to mind. *Oh my god! She gave her life to save me!* The thought of this hurt her deeply. *Wait...am I dead or alive?* The pictures continued to play in her mind while her eyes scanned the room watching everything, cautiously but curious. She could see other shapes in the room were people, not angels. Well, at least that told her she wasn't dead. Watching, she realized these other people were separated in another room, observing all that was going on. This room was like nothing she had ever seen before! The lights were coming from everywhere—out of the ceiling, out of the walls, there were lights coming out of the floor! She heard a weird sound, almost like someone breathing hard and laborious. Turning, she searched around the area near her and saw a pump next to the bed. Lights were even flashing from the pump! Flashing red and green, pressing up and down.

With a lingering glance and squinted eyes, she turned to the man next to her and asked, "How do you know me? I've never seen you before?"

I don't understand anything going on. But one thing for sure, I am going to find a way out of here, she thought to herself as she brushed her hand across her lap.

She gasped. Looking down, she saw only a thin sheet covering her body. Her cheeks burned with heat. Reaching out, she pressed her fingers to her face. "Oh, my God. I don't have any clothes on! I'm naked. I feel awful! Please do something!" Reaching to cover her breast with her hands, she saw a needle attached to a clear tube. The only other time a needle had been put in her arm was when the doctor gave her a small pox shot. *Why was this one still stuck my arm?* Melissa screamed out in panic, "Ahh! What the—Oh, God! What are you doing to me?"

She dropped the sheet around her waist and reached out to jerk the clear tube out of her arm.

The doctor reached out and quickly grabbed her wrist before she could cause damage to her arm. He held tightly, not letting go.

"Please, calm yourself, Melissa. Give me time to explain. Just don't pull your IV out."

Still scared, she turned her head away.

"Melissa, don't be anxious, it's all right."

She felt him waiting for her. When she turned, he could see she was upset and afraid. Tears and fear were filling her eyes, but she bravely looked back at him. He could tell she did not trust him, her emotions were riding high, and he was not equipped to handle humans at this level.

"Melissa, I'm stepping away. I apologize, I didn't mean to frighten you, okay? I'm stepping back now. So please do not pull the IV from your arm, you'll only cause harm to yourself."

After she nodded again, he stepped away from the bed to stand in front of her. He slowly touched her hands now folded in her lap and cautiously picked up the sheet from around her waist. She became rigid at his touch, and her eyes followed his movements while he pulled it around her shoulders to conceal her body from everyone's view. Awkwardly, he patted her shoulder before releasing her.

"Melissa, you know you're in a lab, and of course we're all doctors whose main job is research, right? You've been injured, so I need to follow through with an exam, just to make sure everything is all right and to ensure there are no internal injuries."

She hesitated for a few seconds then nodded. Melissa was nervous and still couldn't understand why or how she came to be here. Not only did the people seem strange, but the place was strange.

Dr. Jacob continued to explain,

"I know this is unusual for you, so it's probably a little frightening. I understand you have many questions." He paused to pat her hands before continuing. "But if you can hold until I can get to them or Dr. Ariella, we'll answer all of them in time, alright?" He assured with raised eyebrows.

Dr. Ariella? Who was that? Melissa wondered. *Please tell me she's not another one like him!* She took another quick look around the room. It was still very bright, but now everyone was gone except for one person. Melissa leaned slightly over to the side to glance around Dr. Jacob. There was a tall woman with long hair, even with it tied back at the nape of her neck. Melissa could see where it hung over her shoulder that it was long. Her hair was auburn with golden highlights. She was very beautiful with green eyes and smooth peach-colored skin.

Dr. Jacob peeked over his shoulder to see where Melissa was looking. "Ah, this is Dr. Emma Ariella. She has been assigned to you as your Watcher. The two of you will get together later on. However, for now, I have an examination to complete on you, Melissa. Dr. Ariella, we'll talk later. Until then, Shalom."

With a curt nod of dismissal, he turned his back, indicating that he was finished with the conversation and her. The doctor nodded, gave a quick glance at Melissa, and smiled before leaving the room.

Melissa thought to herself as Dr. Ariella left, *Dr. Ariella seemed a bit different. Maybe warmer than Dr. Jacob. Even though he does try to be nice, it just doesn't work, and he isn't the most comfortable person to be around with.* Her eyes slowly closed as she drifted to sleep.

Dr. Jacob thought his primary interest at that point was to complete the examination on Melissa. She was strong willed and strong minded with a very strong personality. While all that is necessary for survival, she will hopefully learn a bit of self-control during training. He pulled his surgical gloves on and prepped for the exam. He couldn't remember the last time he'd interacted so closely, for that length of time, with a human female. As a Seeker, he just didn't relate very well with humans at any level really. It just wasn't one of his strong suits.

Several hours later, Melissa woke up. Looking around the sterile, cold room, she thought to herself, *How detached this room felt. Even the smell in the room was lifelessness.* She saw the surgical instruments on the table across the room; something about them looked so impersonal. Scanning the room, she could not see one thing that made her feel comfortable; even the dimmed lights can't shut out the harshness in the room. Not even the soft droning of the machines could make it feel softer. Nothing diminished the eeriness in this place. Melissa rubbed her hands up and down the outside of her arms, trying to warm herself. She felt a stabbing pain in her left forearm. Looking down, she saw a huge purple bruise on the inside of her arm, and the stitches were still in her left side. She was exhausted. Exhaling, she closed her eyes and slumped against the pillow wondering, *Where am I? Mom, Dad, is all of this a bad dream? Am I going to wake up and find y'all in the kitchen? Mom, you'll be cooking breakfast on the stove while dad's out cleaning his gun, getting ready to go hunting?* Tears slid down her cheeks as she studied the IV still fixed in her arm. Reaching across with her right hand, she touched the needle. *The achy soreness.* Closing her eyes, memories came sliding back into her mind. She felt… demoralized! Yep, that's the word she was looking for, that's how she felt. How else could one explain this feeling? Like a piece of leftover meat no one wants. *The doctor had finished his examination. I'm left in this room with nothing except this thin sheet,* she thought!

Emma Ariella watched Melissa through the glass door from across the room. She thought to herself, *No young girl should have to go through what this girl has had to endure. Worse still, she's going to have to go through even more. She's only sixteen years old. Devastated after seeing her mother's throat cut and her father shot. What a way to learn that life holds no guarantee or promise of tomorrow.* Her job now is to help Melissa put her life back together, be her trainer, her Watcher, support her as she brings her to an understanding that places like this strange laboratory will be a part of her life.

As Emma stood there contemplating her role, she thought of how she was going to explain all this to a teen who has traveled 153 years into the future. Sure, she was still sixteen—plus 153 years! Maybe she wasn't your average teen anymore, now that she was actually 169 years old, and she was going to travel *even further* into the future, learn even more about the world than what her eyes could see! Emma stepped forward through the doors as they opened and then closed behind her. She walked to where Melissa was propped back against her pillow. *Well here goes,* she said quietly in her mind.

"Melissa, would you like to get dressed?" Emma asked.

Melissa's jaw tightened in annoyance. She was already perturbed about her arm. *Honestly! Who wants to sit around—naked—in a strange place like this?*

she thought. But she didn't. *Her mother raised her better than that, just like all southern families—with the best of manners.*

"Yes, please. I'm kind of cold," she said as she wrapped her arms around herself and sat up. "I don't mean to be rude, but…are you just now thinking of my wardrobe? And why haven't you given me something besides this sheet?"

Emma could hear the frustration in Melissa's soft southern voice. "I do apologize. Even though Dr. Jacob is top in his field, he does have a tendency to focus exclusively on his interest and forgets everything else. His interest at this time was your conditional-behavioral examination," she explained as she walked over and placed some clothing next to her. She worked hard to keep the smile from her lips. She recalled from previous research how important traditions were to the southern people. Showing respect to their elderly and "minding your manners" were two of the most important ones on the "southern agenda."

Melissa removed the disposable cap covering her hair. While leaning over to pick up the small pile of clothes next to her, she listened to Emma talk. Quickly running her hands over the coarseness of the jeans, she then slowly touched the soft blue-checked cotton shirt with appreciation, enjoying the feel of the material.

"When it comes to everyday life and the things that people need to live… well… Dr. Jacob just doesn't seem to be able to 'connect the dots.'" Emma smiled. "You know. Make a connection or understand the importance of doing so."

Melissa's top lip curled up and her eyes squinted. *Yeah, he thinks I'm a bug,* she thought.

"Um, you don't have dresses? I mean all the best-dressed women wear dresses, not blue jeans. These are used to work in. Why are you giving me work wear? I don't understand."

Emma smiled. "Melissa, here on this island we do things a little differently. If you'll just trust and go along with me, I promise you I won't lead you wrong. I promise I'll also explain everything to your satisfaction, okay?"
Looking down, she reached for the plastic bag. She looked up and nodded then stretched inside the plastic bag to pull out the clothes. She pulled out white panties and bra.

"Wow! I love this!" she said, pointing at the bra. "My mother was going to buy me one, we had already ordered one from the catalog. Thank you!" she said as she hugged the bra close to her chest. Just for a second everything else was forgotten.

Emma nodded her head in acknowledgement, recalling from her research again that in many of the old small southern towns during economically hard times, women didn't have access to this garment, so this would be a wonderful gift for Melissa.

Walking over to Melissa's bed, she held out her hand. "Melissa, let me help you. Hold still for a second while I take the IV out. It'll be sore for the next few days, but the purple should fade soon."

She worked quickly, pulling the needle out of her arm while applying oil to the bruised area. Melissa noticed writing on the bottle, "Skin Oil E." She watched Emma closely as she finished up her work and threw everything into a white cloth bag supported by a silver, hooped-shaped pole. Walking over, she turned off the pump and turned on a lamp.

"There's a room where you'll be staying until we can find something better."

"Wait, can't I go home? I… I mean, I don't want to stay here!"

Emma held her hand up. "Melissa, we really need to talk first. Until that happens, you'll have to stay inside. You can't even leave the building. I don't know how to better explain it to you except to say that in our discussion, I'll be updating you on more than just the rules of the island. Can we leave it at that for now? I will say one more thing, I have some difficult things to go over with you about you and your family."

Melissa slid off the bed and came to stand in front of Emma, her hands curled in fists, her nails digging into her palms.

"Look, I really don't know what you and your Dr. Jacob are doing or even what the rest of those people are doing, but I'm tired of all this. I don't understand what's going on and I don't really care. I want to go home! I'm trying hard to be the person my mother raised me to be, but you're not making this easy. This place is a nightmare, it's creeping me out!"

"Okay, I can understand that. Get dressed and I'll have someone escort you to a set of rooms where we can eat lunch and discuss plans and options, then we'll see where things go from there, how about that?"

Melissa stood silently for a few seconds, thinking, and then nodded in agreement as she turned back to her clothes, waiting for the doctor to leave. Melissa felt a little awkward in jeans and a blue-checkered cotton top. She was used to wearing dresses, but these pants felt comfortable so she guessed she could get used to wearing them. She looked down at her feet—black shoes softly padded on the inside, she wiggled her toes. The material on the outside, she was told, was designed to allow air to pass through the sole of the shoe to keep her feet fresh and full of energy. Her hair was brushed and falling straight down her shoulders. Looking in the mirror, she reached back and pulled her hair up high into a ponytail, making her look even younger than her sixteen years.

The automated doors slid silently open. Melissa turned to see two men standing in the opened doors. They had on dark sunglasses and midnight blue turbans, the same color as the long coats they wore. The coats were clasped around their necks and hung from their shoulders to the floor. They were buttoned one inch apart and hidden by an overlap of material, from top to bottom. They wore flat-soled rubber shoes. The men escorted Melissa from the room across to a wide entrance way, where a large circular stairway was shaped like half-moons stacked on top of each other. Descending the stairs, they came to a large opened foyer filled with people dressed in all colors and fashions. She had not seen anything like this in her life, people were going in all directions; Melissa was impressed by the whole scene! She felt a warm hand touching her lightly on the arm. Twisting to look, she found her escorts motioning for her to follow them. Following along behind, watching their turbans bob up and down through the crowd, she suddenly noticed her shoes were touching smooth stones. Looking down, she saw soft, warm, blue colors of different shades from one corner of the room to the other all throughout the foyer. It looked as if she were walking on water. She was amazed—never in her life had she seen such beauty! Her escorts steered her through the crowd into a sitting room off to the far right, away from the noise and bright lights. It seemed like an oasis of peace and quiet inside the cozy sitting room.

"This is the sitting room Dr. Ariella has reserved for the two of you. Please," Ruben said as he gestured with his hand for her to enter the room. Looking around, Melissa saw that it was dark toward the back of the room where the walls were built of heavy brick. In the center of one of the brick walls was a large fireplace. In front of the fireplace was a small dinner table with four chairs. All around the rest of the sitting room were plush sofas and chairs arranged for comfort, and a large bar with drinks and eating delicacies of all types. Across the room leading out on to the island's large estate was another set of large folding doors to the left of the exit that lead on to a large balcony with a beautiful view of an enormous Indoor Aero Garden.

"Wow! I've heard about these gardens before, but I've never seen one. Can I..."

Turning to question her escorts, she was embarrassed to find herself alone. Not paying attention, she put her hand over her mouth and glanced around the room to see if anyone noticed her blunder, but there was no one there. Again, she felt she was falling behind. She kept wanting to ask, Where am I? Melissa sensed she had fallen down that rabbit hole after all! "Melissa, I'm glad to see that Ruben and Foster were able to escort you here in time. With all the crowds and the celebration going on, I was afraid you might've gotten lost in the crowd."

Melissa jumped, surprised to see Dr. Ariella walk toward her. *Wasn't I the only one in the room?* She was dressed in a pale blue off-shoulder gown, with a diamond necklace around her neck. Her hair was pulled up on top of her head. She was beautiful, her cheeks and lips were the color of strawberries and she had a little sparkle in her eyes. Melissa felt like such a klutz and very underdressed! She had just run a brush through her hair and had piled it on top of her head; she felt drab compared to the doctor. "Um…yes, I'm here. We were supposed to talk about…um, can we get started?"

Emma could hear the sensitivity in Melissa's voice and knew she was uncomfortable. "Melissa, let's sit down over here where it's quiet. I reserved this room so we shouldn't be disturbed. We have a few issues to go over, so we may as well eat while we're talking. Come on." Waving her hand, she invited Melissa to join her at the dinner table.

"Let's start at the beginning. Do you remember when Dr. Jacob first introduced me to you?" She asked as she pulled the dinning chair out. At Melissa's nod Emma continued. "Do you remember how he introduced me?"

Melissa sat there for a minute. Shaking her head, she shrugged her shoulders. "What difference?"

"It's important, think about it. Tell me what you remember." "Well, yes, he called you my Watcher, what did he mean?"

Looking at Emma, she thought, *I did think that was a little odd, but, well, considering where I was at the time, 'odd' did seem to be the theme for the program.* "Dr. Ariella, I don't really know what to ask, except to say, why Watcher?"

"Good question, where should I start? Feel free to interrupt when you've got a question, or don't understand something. This can get confusing, so it's really important that you keep track."

After eating their meal, they headed for the sofa. Melissa plopped down on the sofa and pulled her right leg up beneath her before laying her arm up along the back of the sofa cushion, making herself comfortable, and got ready to hear the story of her mother's life.

"I want to give you a little bit of history, but I don't want to overload you with too much information. Okay. History records tell us that somewhere around 100 AD, everyone was pretty much in touch with their personal self, who they were and who they believed in, as in the Creator, the Ancient of Days, the Great I Am, and many other names He is known by. Up until this time, everyone looked to the Creator for guidance. But as time moved along and as the human race grew, the less they looked to the Creator for direction. Instead, they became full of pride and sought out other means of approval. This was all the chief god Amon-Re needed to hear. He had always been jealous of the Ancient of Days. He saw his opportunity and took it. Soon, Amon took over and ruled the hearts of humankind. Then came the realization that the world had lost its faith in the One who created it. Fewer men devoted themselves to the calling of the priesthood. This being so, a small band of priests, whose hearts still belonged strongly to their Creator and all that he had gifted them with, decided to form a small priesthood called the Seekers. The Seekers worked for many years keeping records such as the arts, history, and science. But the problem came when the Seekers started losing touch with mankind. They were no longer able to communicate with them or even understand their needs or emotions. So they formed a small sect called the Watchers. That's where we came in, Melissa."

"Seekers, Watchers, I don't understand. What's the difference again?"

"Keep listening, I'll bring it all together for you. The Seekers are an ancient Order that ordained a small secret sect called the Watchers. The Seekers are human beings who travel through time. However, they are not your average human beings, they have special gifts from the Creator Himself. These gifted humans are the Record Keepers, Historians, Observers of Life, and Event Keepers. Most Seekers don't interact with humans and live their whole lives on the sidelines. They are gifted at all levels and degrees with spiritual gifts. However, not all Seekers have the same gifts or are as gifted as others. There are only a few Seekers that are unusually gifted to the point that they are free to choose their journey in life. They may choose to remain Priests and Seekers or join the small sect of Watchers. Most of those who join this sect are extremely gifted individuals."

"Wait a minute!" Melissa spoke up. "What's the difference… don't they do the same thing, aren't you and Dr. Jacob the same? Don't you both work as doctors?"

"It's a little more complicated than that. Dr. Jacob is a Seeker who studied in the field of physiology; I'll explain that to you later. Right now I want to explain to you what I do. The Watcher is also human. However, he or she has a lifespan that can last anywhere from two hundred to five hundred years."

Melissa looked at Emma with eyes full of wonder. "Dr. Ariella, can I ask? Are you, like really old?"

Emma laughed. "Melissa, I think by now you can start calling me Emma, right? Which reminds me, when our people give birth, we have a special naming ceremony eight days after the birth of the baby. When the parents give their baby a name, it's a name that will depict the personality of the child for the rest of their life. My name 'Emma' means complete, united, or universal healer."

Melissa thought about it for a moment and then nodded.

"Over the years, the Watchers have been allowed to become more personable. We've been allowed to interact with the average human so that we can be more in touch with life. However, it's always been advised that we shouldn't make commitments or form any close attachments with them because this causes undue stress and distractions; it also interferes with the main objective. A Watcher's main objective is to keep watch over the human population to ensure their protection during harmful situations, making an appearance when necessary—offering aid, in general, keeping the balance within humanity."

Melissa thought about that as she twirled her finger through her hair. "How does one choose to become a Watcher?" she asked.

"Another good question. When a Seeker reaches the ages of fifteen to twenty, he or she can choose to remain in the life of a Priest and Seeker or join the sect of Watchers. However, only the Seeker with at least one or more of these spiritual gifts has the ability to make the choice. Those gifts are: second sight, gift of healing, or the gifts in the area of discernment such as telepathy. The Record Keepers, Historians, Observers of life, and Event Keeper are still the responsibilities of the Seekers. The thing is, the average human cannot see the Priests and Seekers, only the Watchers are able to see them; but that's a conversation for another time, okay?"

Emma studied Melissa as she reached over to pour coffee into their cups. Trying to guess Melissa's emotions from her facial expressions was like trying to catch fish from a barrel, it was not an easy task. Melissa was not an easy card to read. She was just like Tessa, everything was always close to the chest.

"I still don't understand what all of this has to do with me. Why are you telling me all of this?"

"Melissa… Tessa—" Emma broke off.

Melissa's eyes widen when she heard her mother's name.

"…she was a Watcher. Her name meant Gatherer."

Melissa slowly pulled her arm away from the sofa. Turning, she put her feet side by side on the floor in front of her. Sliding to the front edge of the sofa, she turned her eyes back in Emma's direction and stared at her. She was confused.

"How did you know my mother? You just said her name. Do you know me from before too?"

Emma sensed her mistrust immediately and her suspicion.

"Tessa was my best friend, Melissa. We went to school together. We spent most of our lives together. As young girls, we were inseparable, doing almost everything together," she explained calmly, trying not to cause her any further upset.

Melissa felt a little strange. Here was a person she had never heard of before, and yet she talked about her mother with such awareness. Her gut told her to be careful. The ambiance in the room changed. She was concerned, she reached out and pulled the cloth of her jeans tightly together before letting it go; once, twice, then a third time. Avoiding eye contact, she focused instead on the movement of her hand as she counted softly to herself in an effort to remain calm. "Did you know my father too?" Her chin jutted forward, her eyes moved toward Emma, but still refused to look at her.

"No, I didn't know James Fuller. I was—" Emma stopped speaking when Melissa snapped her head around, as if daring her to continue. She felt as if Melissa was reading her mind.

"You knew, didn't you? You knew they were in danger? Why didn't you save them?" Melissa cried. "Why did you just watch them die!" She slapped her hand over her mouth, and with an exaggerated huff of breath, she said sarcastically, "Of course, how could I forget? You're a Watcher!" She taunted. "You just watch…you don't do anything. What good are you to anyone except for writing things down on paper!?" Melissa's teeth were clenched tightly together as she struggled to get her words out, shooting them at Emma like arrows. But she was so emotionally charged, her words came out slurred.

Emma had to listen closely to understand anything she said. But there was nothing she could say, no comfort she could give that would help Melissa understand things the way they really were. *How do you explain to someone who has always lived life in a three-dimensional world, where length, width, and height is just common place? How do you explain that there are people who live and interact in dimensions that this one hasn't heard of, that there are time-travelers who live in a world where time travel is the norm and has always been a way of life? How does one tell a sixteen-year-old about the Order of the Seekers who live in a four-dimensional world, the same world where Tessa and I have been, and it is still a part of my life style? The shock this poor girl is about to go through when she realize there is actually more than this present time, more possibilities than the world she lived, breathed, traveled, and loved!* These thoughts raced through Emma's mind reminding her of all that Melissa has to absorb. So she remained silent to allow her time to grieve for her parents. Emma's heart ached for her. Finally, she stepped forward and spoke.

"Melissa, I know it's hard to understand. There's nothing I can say that will help to heal your heart. Only time will do that. However, I will explain who your mother was and how I knew of your father, alright?"

By now, Melissa was leaning forward. Her shoulder hunched as her hands covered her face. She wept as if her heart were too heavy for her chest. Nodding, she agreed to listen.

"Your mother was a Watcher just like me. We're here to help keep and restore balance to humanity and to keep our personal views and opinions out of everything we do. The history, science, or human events that are recorded cannot reflect our thoughts or personality. If we were to get too close, we would no longer be able to see both sides objectively. We're not here to take sides; instead, we're here to ensure that history and the future remains uninterrupted. We are time travelers, we go in and out of time like the average human goes in and out of elevators from one floor to the next. The only time we can step in and interrupt the flow of time is when the evil forces come and tries to rewrite history from what the Creator intended in the beginning or tries to create a future that will write out a person the Creator has considered for an important role somewhere in time he or she is meant to play out. That's when we have to step in and protect the bloodline of that person, so they'll not be written out of the Record of Life."

Melissa held her hand up in the air, giving it a little shake. "You said that you, the Watcher, are advised not to get involved with humans or make commitments of any kind. So, how did my mother get involved with my father?"

Emma sighed. "Well, I knew that question was coming, but still it's a hard one to answer. Tessa and I were assigned to the same fire team. We traveled back in time on an assignment to investigate a murder involving a family who were supposed to have died out long before our time. The last of their line, hypothetically, was to have ended right after the Vietnam War. However in our time during the mid-3,000s, a murder happened which was traced back to the late 1800s, during James's time and his family tree. When your mother first met James, he had no idea who or what she was."

Emma reached out for Melissa's hand.

Melissa laid her hand in Emma's and slowly sat back against the cushions, letting her other arm fall along the side of her body while she gradually relaxed in slow stages and listened to Emma tell the story of her mother's life.

"When Tessa and James first met, she was posing as a nurse in a clinic in Resaca, Georgia. The clinic was set up to aid and care for the wounded soldiers on both sides of the battle. James was one of the officers in command of a small group of men General Johnston had planted in Resaca, just as he had done so in several other small towns to keep guard over the townspeople during times when the fighting was most intense. James and Tessa started talking. At first, she was just getting information about his family, trying to find a point and place in the bloodline where everything started going wrong. This way, maybe…just maybe…we could get an idea where our investigation needed to pick up. However, the more she grew to know him and his family, the more she fell headlong in love with him, and, of course, his parents. When he asked her to marry him, she accepted." Emma shrugged. "I don't believe he ever knew what she gave up for him when she became his wife."

Melissa turned her head, her face had a frown. "What do you mean, 'gave up'?" she asked with a sneer.

"Well, you remember what I said about Watchers not getting involved with the average human, right?" At Melissa's nod, she continued.

"When Tessa married James, she gave up her rights to have an active Watcher's lifestyle. Of course, she was born to this so she would always be a Watcher, but she could no longer be a part of our team or communicate with us or her family. That was a great sacrifice on her part, which just goes to show how much she loved your father. When they got married she had to stop the investigation. She did break the rule for one exception—when she had you. As you grew up she realized that you were a Watcher and that you were extraordinarily gifted, some of which she had passed along to you herself. Anyway, I'm sure you do know that Tessa and James loved each other very much; it was a strong love, especially on Tessa's part. I'll tell you more about that as we go along. Anyway, Tessa was born in the year of 2940. She was from your future."

Melissa stirred at this, her imagination swirled with bright colors as she stared off into the future. Would she ever see her mother again? Was that possible? She could only hope, maybe catch a glimpse of her somewhere in the future. One parent from the past and one from the future. What did that make her?

"When Tessa and I were born, our world was peaceful; but when our parents were young, the earth was full of evil. The humans had fought almost to the brink of extinction. The world had been ravaged by war. All major cities had been destroyed, leaving small groups of people spread throughout the earth. It was at this point the Watchers joined the humans as they fought along beside them to help bring an end to their fighting and bring peace and harmony once again to the human race. As the feeling of peace overcame the people, they started rebuilding settling into small villages, farmlands, and homesteads. As a result of the rebuilding, the humans soon discovered that not everything in the old world had been destroyed; there were strong communications and satellite systems still in place."

Emma went on to explain how the Priests had fought hard for the humans to have and enjoy peace. At last, an end to war had finally come during their lifetime, or so they all thought. There was tranquility for the first time in hundreds of years. It had been prophesied and written in the old scrolls and manuscripts, "There will come a time of harmony when wars and rumors of wars will cease, when all chaos will come to an end, and all will be at peace. When all beings will live in one accord, as was in the beginning when the Creator started all creation." The humans began to colonize in a place known as Arkay. It was beautiful. A river curved and flowed through the middle of the land for miles. The Seekers settled into their individual territories. During this peaceful season, Tessa and I were born. By this time, the humans had made their homes all throughout the lower lands of Earth while the Watchers lived in the area once inhabited by Native Americans. The history records called them the Pueblos. Their homes were in the mountains and caves. The Seekers lived in the fourth dimension above the mountains in an area they named Fourth Corner Plateau, and they're still there to this day. The Seekers continue to keep the records of analytical science, biology, history, and life events. The Priests, or as they're called the Order of Seekers nowadays, worked hard for many generations, and they felt this was their time. They could finally relax and be at peace. Emma smiled as the memories stirred around in her mind. She closed her eyes and let her mind slip back in time.

"Tessa was my best friend. There wasn't a time when we weren't together. We went to Academy together and finished our military training together as well! We both were blessed with many gifts, which meant we could serve in the same order for the rest of our lives. I was so excited, both of us were! Life was good, and we saw only happiness in our future and maybe a special someone out there for us one day; maybe marriage, a family. Who knew?"

Turning toward Melissa, her smile held many memories, her eyes studied Melissa's as she leaned forward and touched her finger to Melissa's hand lying on her lap. Patting her hand, she stood up and stretched, interlacing her finger above her head and giving her arms a long stretch. Melissa, still sitting on the sofa, closed her eyes as a clear vision of her mother came to mind. She wanted to escape into this world; it made her feel better hearing about her mother, knowing that she enjoyed her life. Also, it gave her a piece of her mother back, if only for a little while.

"I remember one of my favorite times of the year, Tessa loved it too. It was the month of Nisan—the month of happiness. This would be on your calendar year, around March or April. I can remember going outside of my home and standing there, looking down the mountainside over the fields where the humans planted their barley. It was like looking at nature's golden carpet spread out across the fields. Those were the days—so amazing, so beautiful! This is how Tessa and I grew up. But as the old, old saying goes, 'All good things must come to an end,' and it eventually did." Emma walked back around the sofa to the bar to get Melissa and herself a glass of sweet tea and some sandwiches. As she prepared a treat for the both of them, she placed napkins and drinks on a tray and walked back over to the sofa and motioned for Melissa to eat.

"I believe it was during the year of 2990 when a restlessness started. It slowly spread among the humans. We didn't really notice it at first, so when it actually started… well, there isn't a record, because we had become complacent and had forgotten to watch the humans—we had forgotten to maintain the balance of humanity.

"The humans had so many feasts and festivals they shared with each other so often without any problems. This time shouldn't have been any different. It was the usual practice each year for everyone from the community village of Verde to contribute to the Spring Festival in celebration of life, the birth of another spring. It wasn't unusual for the farmers or neighbors to leave his or her portion of supplies out to be collected by whoever came around to pick up the contributions. But this time was a little strange. The young man who gathered supplies from all the farmers for the Spring Festival was going around, doing the usual gathering of supplies. I believe it was the Taylors who hosted the Verde Festival that year. Anyway, they were getting supplies from everyone.

"On this particular night the Taylor boy came to Michael Folks's barn, and for some reason Michael grew angry and jumped out and swore violently at the boy and started screaming to the top of his voice. 'Who in the name of Osiris do you think you are? Walking into my barn like that and stealing from me? Now go on, get outta here before I shoot you where you stand!' He pulled a rifle from beneath his workbench and cocked it, waiting while the young boy just stood there looking at Michael in confusion, not really understanding what was going on, more shocked than anything. Embarrassed and confused, he dropped the supplies and ran out of the barn. Later, Michael apologized, even though he didn't explain why he'd gotten angry, but to show how badly he felt he brought an extra basket of supplies to the festival."

Melissa pulled her hands up behind her head. "That kind of thing happens all the time where I come from, why would that bother anybody? I don't understand," she said shaking her head.

"Well, it had been peaceful for so long and, suddenly out of nowhere, this happened after all this time, and now it looked as if no one in the community trusted each other the way they did in the past. The Commanding Watchers called for an alert once again, and each Watcher was put on alert more often than before. Something seemed to be stirring in the air. The villages didn't trust each other. The tension could be felt in the air. There was a definite difference in the pattern of life, changes were stirring within the humans' behavior; it was unmistakable and very distinguishable."

Emma went on to describe the events of the Verde Spring Festival and why this year was so important. The Seekers were hoping the humans would be able to bring some reconciliation among them. The village of Verde gave the impression that it was ready for a day of feasting—everything was a picture of brightness and beauty, just perfect for a day of celebration! All the villagers from the surrounding small towns and communities were bringing their food and other local offerings for the opening day of festivals to celebrate spring and the birth of new beginnings. As always, there were native art shows, and also family and friends attending who had not been seen in ages. It was a time of renewal of family members, of friendships and contracts between businesses. The music could be heard for miles. Emma grinned. Hundreds of pictures came and went of precious memories forever gone.

With a sigh she turned to Melissa.

"Like I said before, this was my favorite time of year! There would be lots of dancing, eating, and much-needed laughter. I remember standing by one of the tables set up to serve sample of the spring wines. While standing there, I saw the people enjoying the festival. I appreciated the beauty of all that surrounded me. Tessa reached out and touched my shoulder as she pointed out the new leaves and the smell of the fresh grass. I always forgot how much I missed that each year, until it came back around the next!" Emma's eyes were fixed on another time. Her expression was full of memories and wonder.

"I remember, Tessa raised her hand up about eye level and spread her fingers out so she could look through them to the sunshine coming through the trees to warm the skin on our arms. Even though it was spring, there was still snow on the mountain tops, so when the wind blew down across the mountains and through the fields, there was a slight chill. Yes, I could feel the emotions that came along with the new life of spring. Yep, I'd missed all of that during those cold winter days."

Emma sat up and slid her shoes back on her feet. She reached over and pulled a thick shawl from the back of the sofa and wrapped it around her as if she could feel the cool breeze from the mountains falling on her shoulders. Sitting up straight, her face became serious. Melissa watched her carefully, wondering at the change in her emotions.

"The festival was drawing to a close; everyone gathered their belongings as they started their journeys home. It had been a good day, everyone had a sense of gratification. It was a good note for departure as everyone left and went their different ways."

Emma tapped her fingers on the table, as if she wanted to stop there. But Melissa could see something else was on her mind.

"What is it, Emma? What happened?"

"Everything was fine until the next morning. While some of the Watchers were preparing to go on duty and others at breakfast in the mess hall, the harmonic alphorns were heard resounding across the Fourth Corner Plateau from the far side of the North Mountain. It was unusual to hear the alphorns so early in the morning. Everyone rushed outside. The squad leaders commanded their teams to stay put but keep alert.

After several hours and several watches had come and gone, instead of going home, many of the Watchers waited around the hall or the guard stations for news. Finally, around evening, word came that the body of a young boy had been found on the Taylor's farmland. It was the same young boy who had collected supplies for the festival the previous day, the one Michael Folks threatened. He was found left in his father's field, face down with no clothes on his body. The clothes that were torn from his body were found about a mile away. There was a large symbol engraved on his back—a circle, and on the inside of the circle his skin was as dark as tar and resembled a piece of wrinkled cowhide, stretched out tightly and dried. Just like the circle, the grass that surrounded the perimeter of his body for three miles around had turned from the lush spring green to a deep dark brown.

"The symbol was the mark of death. It had not made an appearance since the times of the ancients—when the Ancient of Days had to come down and deal with Death himself! This disturbed the Seekers for the simple reason that it had been ages since this sign had made an appearance. The Priests called a meeting to discuss their next step, should there be one. It was decided that an investigation of Michael Folks be completed; maybe an investigation of the entire Folks family, since the threats was aimed at the Taylor boy. The Seekers came together to select an investigation command team."

"What are they going to investigate and why? What's going to happen to that family, what's their name… Folks? How do the Seekers know this has anything to do with them?" Watching Emma, Melissa brought up her two feet together on the cushion, sole to sole, knees bent holding them together, close and tight between her legs with her hands, and waited in anticipation for the answer.

"Mister Taylor's son was threatened by Michael Folks who didn't seem to have a good reason for the threat, plus it seemed to be the most logical place to start. Anyway, I'm getting a little ahead of myself. One evening, around sunset, while the counsel of Seekers was meeting, a little girl named Sandy Doreen was playing in the backyard of her house when she heard a purring noise. Taking a quick look around, she couldn't find anything so she kept playing, even though the purring noise continued to grow louder. Finally, Sandy got up and walked toward the sound, looking around as she went. She brushed the dirt from her hands down along the sides of her dress. Soon her eyes located the spot where the noise was coming from, the wood fence at the back of the yard. She started toward the loud purring sound, which seemed to grow louder the closer she got. When she got to the fence, Sandy peeked through the wooden slats where she saw, to her amazement and wonder, the most beautiful princess she had ever seen, just like the one from her fairytale story. Her hair was a thick chocolate brown color, with curls that cascaded down her back. She wore a gorgeous blue silk evening dress with silver stars interwoven from her neck to her waistline. Sandy's eyes shined with wonder, her little lips trembled with excitement as they formed a perfect 'O' of appreciation. She was in awe of this beautiful creation who seem to have a golden glow about her. As Sandy watched, she was surprised to see a narrow black line appear at the center of the lovely girl's head. What was that? She pressed her face deep into the crack between the wooden slats of the fence. It's started to unpeel from the center, just like when you peel away the outside skin to reveal the fruit inside. Underneath all that beauty, it was black with deep darkness; gray smoke began to roll upward and then swell as the steam poured out, the odor smelled like sulfur. Sandy's eyes grew wide when a set of horns, one on each side of its head poked through the surface. She whispered 'gross' when she saw that the head was covered with tiny white bumps, as the slimy skin slipped away."

Emma shook herself as she continued with her story. "The rest of the body showed then. The fingers on the creature's hands, the tips of each finger were red like branding irons, and just like its head, its hands were white and covered in tiny white pimply bumps. Sandy stood still with fear. Even though she couldn't see the front of the body, the back view was enough! She quickly covered her mouth with both hands to keep from screaming, and stumbled as she ran back to her house. Once she was there and safely inside with her parents, she stood still trembling inside the doorway. Her parents turned to see her standing there staring at them, shaking. Sandy's mother asked what was wrong, but she fainted and dropped to the floor. When she came back around, they asked her what had happened but she wasn't able to speak or explain. So her parents called for the Priests, who then sent for Tessa. Tessa asked me to join her. Since we were a team, I decided to go along to the Doreen's home. The Priests called for Tessa because she was gifted with telepathy. When we went inside, Sandy was lying on the sofa with her parents sitting by her side. The Seekers were watching from Laptec on my laptop, from the coffee table in the living room.

Melissa looked at Emma, her forehead wrinkled in question. "Laptec? Laptop?"

Emma waved her hand at her, "I'll explain later. Tessa walked in and went over to Sandy. She placed her right index and middle fingers on Sandy's left wrist pulse, then she put her left thumb next to Sandy's ear. Her left index and middle fingers were on Sandy's forehead. She then began to read her thoughts and displayed the images on the laptop. This is how we know the details of what actually happened that evening in Doreen's backyard."

Emma turned and gathered the sandwiches and drinking glasses as her assistant approached. She motioned for him to gather everything so that she could finish talking with Melissa.

"Once the details were recorded by Tessa, the counsel of Priests again met with a few of the Seekers to record the visions Tessa viewed from Sandy's mind. Once the Seekers completed their meeting, they saw the gravity of the situation and decided to meet with the Human Renaissance Committee to discuss the next steps to be taken to prepare Earth for the impending war. This was not something the Seekers were going into lightly. It seemed the door had been closed on this issue. However, the Creator was allowing other things to come into our flow of life that was opening the doors of war once again. As I said before, the cause of this war came from a very old bloodline that should have been destroyed thousands of years ago, but somehow survived. The Priests requested that Tessa and I go along with this Fire Team to conduct an investigation. We weren't excited about the war, but we were excited to be involved in a mission. This was our time, this is what we had been training for all these years, and finally we were going on a mission! Little did we understand how this would change our lives, our friendship, and our futures forever."

Emma stood and stretched again before turning back to look at Melissa. Her hands were resting on her hips, her eyes were sad. That moment looked to Melissa it looked as if she had the eyes of the ancients, eyes that had seen too many years with too many losses.

"Melissa, this is a lot to take in. I know I promised to tell you all about Tessa and I will, but, first, I want to give you time to absorb the rest of what's been said. Write down any questions you can think of, and I'll try and answer them tomorrow when we pick up right where we left off. We'll talk about the investigation and the shape-shifter, which is what Sandy saw in her backyard. Right now, I know if I'm tired you've got to be. So why don't we call it a night? We have some heavy stuff to cover tomorrow. I'll send for you in the morning. We'll eat breakfast and talk. See you in the morning!"

Just as she was turning to leave, she spun around and said, "Hey! I'm going to send you more clothes and shoes. A girl can't have too many shoes! I'll let Ruben and Foster escort you back to your rooms. You'll be in a different set of rooms tonight. I think you'll like them. If you do, you can stay there until we leave." Emma gave her the thumbs up sign and waved good-bye as she turned.

Melissa stood up, stretched, and fell into step between Ruben and Foster who took her out to the foyer to a large elevator where the doors slid silently open, allowing the three of them to step inside. There were two large sofas, one on each side. The elevator was more like a large living room than an elevator. Three of the walls were of cream color. The back wall was all glass.

Once again, Melissa was amazed at all the new things she saw while strolling over to look down through the glass wall. She watched as the elevator quickly shot upward. Startled, she stood still. Her eyes wide as saucers as she watched the elevator leaving the ground behind and then, just as smoothly, it came to a quick standstill. The door swiftly slid opened to allow Melissa and her escorts to exit. She stood there shaking her head back and forth, willing herself back to reality.

Ruben and Foster walked Melissa to her set of rooms. Ruben stepped forward and unlocked the door before turning to hand her the keys, then he and Foster left. She gently eased the door open and walked into a large extravagant three-room suite where she found a living room with a full sofa area, fireplace, loveseat, and two sofa chairs. There was a large flat picture frame hanging on the wall. Melissa walked up close to it, but there was nothing there but an empty frame, no picture.

She moved toward the window, touching the heavy, dark red material where a sheer fabric piece hung inside between the two curtains. Pulling the fabric back away from the window, she realized it wasn't a window at all but a door. Hesitating, she slid the door open on to a spacious balcony overlooking a garden. It was beautiful. The only thing she could really see outside was the large full moon peeking out from behind the clouds. There didn't seem to be many lights on the island, at least not any that she could see. Walking back inside, she went into the bedroom where a large king-size bed sat. The whole bedroom's décor was a luxurious alpine and extremely spacious. There were two nightstands on each side of the bed, each table had a tall white lamp with a golden lampshade, and the comforter was gold and black. Melissa continued into the bathroom where she found the floors were made of dark green marble. The bathtub was a thick white marble lined around the sides with the same dark green marble as the flooring. There were all kinds of amenities, including a refrigerator, work desk, and other things that Melissa had never seen before. She was amazed by it all and wondered how she would ever get to sleep that night. Later that evening, there was a knock on the door. A chest full of clothes had arrived, as Emma promised. She looked over the fashion magazines Emma provided and hunted for an outfit for the next day. After her shower, she jumped into her pajamas and climbed into bed. But sleep didn't seem to be her friend that night, she finally gave up. Her mind ran swiftly with the stories Emma had told her earlier. Things like "shape-shifter" came to mind. What did Emma mean by that?

Looking around, Melissa reached out and turned the lamp on. She saw a dictionary sitting on top of the desk across the way; she slipped out of bed, grabbed the book, and looked through it to the word shape-shifter. "One that seems able to change form or identity at will." *Change form? Did that mean what she thought? Emma was talking about a presence that appeared to be angelic yet changed to a demonic creature? What exactly was going on here?* Melissa ran over to the other side of the desk and found a tablet and pen and wrote down her first question. "What is a shape-shifter?" Second question quickly followed. "Are we talking about angles and demons? And if we are, how deep are you taking me into this world? Just who was my mother, and did you say she could read other people's thoughts when necessary? What does that mean?" When Melissa looked down at her tablet, she found her notebook full of questions and other thoughts she had written down to ask Emma. Finally, as she trudged back to bed, she felt sleep calling to her. Her dreams were filled with images and words that were strange to her. She was restless, and even though she slept all night it was not a restful one.

The next morning Melissa stretched and yawned her way out of bed and into the shower. She stood with her head bent slightly forward beneath the steamy hot sprays of the water. The warm droplets slid down along her arms and back, the steam came up to meet her face clearing away her foggy memory. She had never experienced a shower before. The future was getting to look better and better. Stretching out, she pushed the shower handle against the wall, turning the water off. Opening the shower door, she grabbed the towel from its hook. The towel felt thick and warm to her body as she breathed in the sundried fragrance and dried herself off. Wrapping it around herself and beneath her arms, she caressed the royal Egyptian cotton fabric. Melissa thought to herself, Mom, *I do miss you and dad. I love you very much, but, boy, do I love some of the things here in the future. This towel is heaven, and that shower is the best, the water is so warm!* She walked over to stand in front of the large bathroom mirror and towel dried her hair. Placing the towel back on the hook, she pulled her hair up on top of her head then looked around to find something to wear. Her closet was now filled with clothes, shoes, and all sorts of things that every teenage girl could wish for. Today, Melissa picked out an off-the-shoulder sundress with the top portion made of thick black lace from the waistline to the neck where the zipper was centered between the breasts to the waist. The skirt portion of the dress was made of blue chiffon fabric, the front was short just above the knees, and the back fell down around the back of the legs to the ankles. She decided to wear a pair of black, ankle-high boots, the heels were flat. To finish the outfit, Melissa chose a combination of silver and black chain necklace, interlaced with smooth gray black stones. Her makeup was a touch of cherry lip gloss. Just as she finished, a knocked sounded at the door. Scooping up her notes from the night before, she ran to answer the door. Swinging it open she saw her faithful escorts Ruben and Foster just on the other side waiting for her. "Good morning, Sirs. How are y'all this morning?" She welcomed them with a smile.

With a slight bow they answered, "Fine, Miss. We're here to escort you to breakfast. Are you ready?" At her nod, Forster held out his arm to escort her through to the foyer. This time there were no crowds or celebrations. Everything was quiet and peaceful. Moving forward, the three of them came to the same sitting room where they met Emma the night before.

"Dr. Ariella will be with you momentarily," Foster said while pulling out her breakfast chair. He signaled for the server to bring her breakfast.

"Miss Fuller, what would you like to eat?" the server asked.

Melissa looked over at the young girl. *She can't be much older than me.* "Please bring me coffee with cream and sugar, also toast and eggs, thank you."

The server left to fill the order while Ruben and Foster said their good- byes and left. Melissa sat down at the table, opened her notebook, pulled her notes from the night before, and began getting ready for Emma.

"Good morning, Melissa. You look beautiful this morning, did you sleep well?"

Looking up, she saw Emma walking toward her, smiling and casually dressed in a yellow sundress with large round dots around the hem below the knees. She wore brown leather sandals. Her fingers and toenails were painted a soft orange color. She looked very relaxed as she called the server over to order breakfast.

After eating breakfast, they talked about the day ahead of them. "Let's go sit over there," Emma suggested, pointing to a couple of recliners on the other side of the room. "Melissa, I think it's about time we do a little visit around the island today. Are you about ready to get outside again?"

Laughing, Melissa relaxed; she knew that whatever was coming she could handle it. Yeah, she was ready! Melissa lifted her right shoulder and smiled. "Yes, I was beginning to think I'd never get to see the sky again." Her nervous laugh gave away her feelings.

"Well, there's a few things we need to talk about first, in case you run up against something you don't understand, I mean."

Melissa got the impression that Emma was trying to say something without actually saying it.

"Okay, Emma, are you trying to tell me I might see something that I haven't seen before? Well, I'm ahead of you. That's been happening since I've been here, so your work's cut out for you."

"Alright, I take it you have questions. So let's get straight to the point. What are they?"

Melissa stuck her chin out toward the conference room window she had been staring out of while eating, pointing her finger toward it. "Well, for one, I know that's not just an enormous bird flying around out there with a huge wing span. See, he just disappeared behind the clouds. He hasn't once flapped his wings. He has to flap his wings or he won't stay up, so…?"

"Remember when you first woke up in the examination room? Remember how afraid you were? You saw the bright lights and then found Dr. Jacob leaning over you? When you looked down and saw the IV in your arm, you were scared stiff, until Dr. Jacob explained to you what was going on?"

"Sure, but what's that have to do with the big bird flying around out there?"

"Well, I'm getting to that. Some of the things I wanted to talk over with you before we walk over the island has to do with all of that. You're going to run into some pretty strange stuff out there. Well, strange to you, anyway. It will be unsettling, I won't lie to you. Some of the explanations I give you won't make a whole lot of sense. But if you'll listen to me and trust me, ask question if you need to, we'll work to bring all of this together and make sense out of it, okay?"

"Okay. So tell me about the bird."

"Okay, that wasn't a bird." Emma smiled a big smile. "That was a plane. Once, long ago two brothers Orville and William Wright made their first successful flight in history on December 17, 1903 near Kitty Hawk, North Carolina, and since then…"

Emma and Melissa sat there for the next hour or so and talked about the laws of aerodynamics. From there, she explained to Melissa about the invention of the first car, or the automobile, by Karl Benz in 1886, that it was called a motor wagon, and the progress that it's made since that time. "Alright, that's just the beginning. Do you have any other questions?

Was there anything in your room that didn't look quite right last night, for example?"

Melissa looked around the room at the walls and the pictures hanging there and the tables with the different pieces sitting around on them. She then turned back to Emma.

"Well…there was something strange in my room. I'm not sure if it's a thing in the future or the present or wherever I am right now. Maybe I'm just missing something. There are two large flat empty frames hanging on my walls, no pictures, empty, why?"

Emma laughed. *Good question*, she thought. *Now, if I can only explain it as good.*

"Well, those aren't picture frames, but they do have something to do with pictures. First, those two large frames are called flat-screen TV. TV is an acronym for television. The first television was invented in the 1920s by a man from Scotland, his name was John Baird. Of course, it was nothing like the big screen you have in your rooms. Back then the box was so small it's a wonder anyone could actually see it at all," she said laughing.

"I'm having a hard time with this. You're talking in the past tense. From my standpoint this is the future. To me it's like make believe, yet, to you, it's a given. So please understand how hard and confusing this is for me." Melissa sighed.

"Oh, Melissa, I'm sorry, I really didn't think of it that way. I know all of this is coming at you so fast, but, unfortunately, we don't have the luxury of slowing down. We've been sent back in time to find you and the others. We have a deadline to reach. That's all I can say right now but I'll do my best to explain as we go along."

Melissa nodded in agreement. "Can I ask one more question?" At Emma's nod, she said, "This is going to sound crazy. I know I must've asked you this before, but… what year is this? 2017."

Melissa sat there quietly and watched while Emma walked across the room to a large flat screen television at the back of the conference room. Picking up the remote control, she turned it on. Immediately the television came alive with voices and faces flashing brightly with news and weather as people talked back and forth with each other. Melissa jumped out of her chair! She stood there for about thirty seconds before running across the room to look behind the television screen. *Nothing.* Then she walked to the door next to the television, opened the door and peeked inside. There was no one. A few seconds later, she walked back out, her eyes full of questions as she looked at Emma.

"Where are they hiding?"

"Come on, let's go sit back down and let me do a little more explaining about our technology."

Emma and Melissa spent another few hours talking about technology. Emma hoped against hope that she could help Melissa catch up with progress and join in on the life and times of today's world so that she could better understand the times she was about to deal with when she finished her training. There was so much to learn in such a short amount of time. After a few hours, Emma thought, *Finally... Melissa is ready to see the world. Well, at least the rest of the island.*

"I'd like you to take a walk across the island to the training facility with me. Ready?"

They walked toward the double doors leading out on to the estate. Melissa's feet sank into thick grassy carpet. The estate was an island set in the middle of a large river where the waters ran rapidly on all sides. Most of the island was surrounded by rock. Emma motioned toward the guard's station. "This is called the North Gate. During the Civil War, the military used to purchase their military equipment here."

Emma saluted the guards as they walked by. "We're headed toward the training facility. This is where all the recruits prepare for battle and begin their first steps in training as Watchers. These are old battle stations, and we believe it's good for our soldiers to be here in the middle of all of this. It helps the morals and spirits of the Watchers as they remember the battles that went on before them."

Melissa came to a standstill in the middle of the path and grabbed Emma's arm.

"Whoa! We're going into battle, we're gonna fight? I… I don't know anything about fighting, nor do I know anything about being a soldier!" "Well, you will when all your training is finished. Tessa was one of the best! Believe me, when I tell you, you will not go into battle unprepared."

"My mother fought in battle? I watched her get killed. She didn't raise her hand once to defend herself!" Melissa shouted, her hands fisted by her sides.

Emma stopped and walked back to her. "There was nothing she could do, Melissa. Tessa had chosen her path a long time ago. She knew what she was doing. Tessa also knew that you were in good hands because she had already sent word for me to come and get you. On the other hand, all we could do was allow history to play its cards."

"What if I'd been raped, stabbed, or, even worse, killed! What's wrong with you people? Don't you value life at all?"

"Wouldn't have happened, we would've stepped in, we were ready and had been put on alert, we were ready to take you."

Melissa was upset and confused. "What was so important that my mother had to send for you?" Tears were now streaming down her cheeks. She was confused. In just a few hours, her mother had become a person she didn't know. She didn't like this and wasn't so sure wanted to be a part of what was going on.

"Because, Melissa, you're very gifted young woman. You inherited the genetic abilities of your mother's people rather than your father's. You see, when Tessa chose a life with James, she chose to give up her life as an active Watcher. Even though, for her, it is hereditary and can never be physically taken away from her. She had to make a choice not to participate or make known to anyone this part of her life. Even though your father wasn't aware of Tessa's abilities, nor was he aware of yours or the fact that as you grew older your skills as a Watcher would surface. Tessa knew, so she did breach just once that part of her unwritten contract, to let us know about you and to keep a watch on you. She knew and understood that one day you would have to leave. Melissa, you're a Watcher."

Melissa did not know what to say. She was stunned and remained quiet as she pondered this new information. Silently, they walked through the old castle. She looked around at some of the old bulkheads and walkways as they walked along. The thick grassy carpet was soon replaced by large flat rocks pieced evenly together like a puzzle. When entering one of the buildings, she noted how the exterior walls seem to stand so strong and proudly tall. However, as they passed through the inside of the building it was easy to see that some of the internal flooring and walls had long ago burnt down. It looked as if parts of the island had been a victim of vandalism, neglect, and decay. She could see where some places in the old building's walls had collapsed. Outside the walls, they walked over several fallen and broken trees which turned into smooth grassy slopes as they climbed up the hill. Melissa could see an old estate home just up the path a way.

"There's the training facility, it's been here since. I would say since around the late 1800s."

At last, they came to an old stone building. The pathway leading up to the building was made of stone. Running alongside the path were about twenty to twenty-five cedar trees. Just behind the cedar trees was a covered walkway leading to a side entrance where a numbered code lock was located. Emma entered the code and the door slid opened. As the door slid close behind Melissa, she examined the interior of the building; it was nothing like she had expected. The first thing she noticed was the floor made of dark limestone which reflected the flashing colors illuminating from the computer positioned at midpoint in the center of the facility. She stood there staring, rooted to the spot, astounded! She became aware of Emma's voice giving details concerning the training area, her voice came from somewhere off in the distance. *My mind… it's in shock*. Melissa laughed to herself. *I know my body's here, but I'm not so sure where my mind is. Maybe it hasn't caught up*. Her eyes and ears followed along as Emma explained in detail. Still, her mind struggled to hold on to what was being said. Emma pointed to the main computer at the center of the room, giving details of how it operated off the energy and thoughts of the Watchers going through training. The Seekers called the computer the "Digital Cortex of Life" or DCL. The computer—a large round flat clear circle that hovered in the air connecting only at two pinpoints, the top and bottom, north and south. As Emma approached the central processing unit, she glanced back at Melissa while stretching her hand out to mimic the turning motion of the computer.

"The circle is in a continuous spinning motion. Inside the circle there is an enneagram which endlessly flashed nine different colors. The Digital Cortex of Life is a constructed nine-point-shaped platform, raised to the leveled height that reaches nine steps on each side at each point of the main frame. Surrounding the Digital Cortex are nine training computers, this is where the recruits receive their combat training. The computers are arranged with seats so the soldiers can sit and position their Digital Dream Processors, or DDP, to cover their head and eyes. The DDP connects to the brain impulses and allows each one to envision themselves in a combat situation.

While in their DDP, the recruits or soldiers who are involved with their learning skills as a Watcher will transcend to the fourth and fifth dimensions which are played out in holograms. However, for the new recruits these holograms can seem very realistic. So, because of their inexperience as Watchers and because traveling to these dimensions are not the usual for the new Watcher as it is for the Seekers, this can be a shock to the new recruit's system, so safety precautions are taken to keep the new recruits fastened in their seats. This is also used as a teaching aid to show just how serious the Watcher's mission is in keeping humanity safe and in balance when fighting alongside other Watchers who fight the demonic forces while in battle."

As Melissa and Emma rounded the corner, seven other recruits were standing just beyond them getting ready for training; four guys and three girls, all within the ages of fifteen and twenty-five. This was the first time Melissa had seen any other persons within her own age range. In the distance she could hear the voices of other commanders.

Emma touched her arm. "Melissa, let's finish your tour and then come back for introductions, alright?" She nodded as they walked back toward the training facility.

"There are nine colored orbs related to the Digital Cortex of Life that continually flash inside the circle. These are the levels of training each recruit will have to complete throughout his or her training experience. As each level is cleared and completed, the color will change and the computer will record the level of training that has been completed. This will allow the team commander to know when recruits have completed their initial training, and when they will be combat-ready."

Walking toward the back of the training facility, Emma and Melissa passed the Digital Cortex Processor and stepped behind the recruit training centers. They rounded the corner coming to a flight of stairs that looped around a pole and went up into the storage space to the top of the building where two large fans whirled nonstop on either side of the upper half of the building. To the right was an exit running off onto a covered catwalk. Melissa followed Emma as they crossed over to a gray green barracks. Once through the door and inside the barracks, she could see five sets of bunks on each side of the building. On the floor was a gray runner that ran the length of the room. Along the floor were two sets of numbers on each side of the bunks. On one side of the room, the numbers were green, and on the other side the numbers were orange. In between each bunk there were two lockers. At the end of the row of bunks and the back of the room was a clothes drop. Just above it was a large flat screen television with a small space just big enough for a small panel. Melissa spun on the backs of her heels as she inspected the barrack.

"This is where you'll probably spend most of your time when you're not training, eating, or studying."

She shrugged her shoulders. "Doesn't sound like much of a life to me."

"Well, since we're not here for social entertainment, this actually is the life for you. You're here to train. By the way, once we're out there I'll be your commander and trainer. So, our relationship will be different; you'll call me Commander Ariella unless we're in the field on a mission. Even so, I'm still the one you'll come to when you need to talk or if you have a problem, alright? Come on let's go meet everyone." They entered the mess hall, a small building across from the barracks with fifteen tables and a chow line. Today, their fireteam was the only one headed in for a meal.

After their meal, Emma stood at the back of the mess hall. "Recruits." Her voice raised. Everyone turned in their seats to face her at the sound of her voice. "I'm Commander Ariella. I'll be your commander through training and your first mission. This evening, there'll be no formalities; however, tomorrow at 0500 you'll consider it the beginning of your official training." Emma lifted her clipboard snuggly to the front of her chest and skimmed down the list of names. "Please stand when you hear your name. Once I've introduced you, take your seat. Recruit Adams, Elizabeth."

A young, eighteen-year-old girl stood up, about five feet six inches tall with brown hair pulled back at the nape of her neck. She had blue eyes and a friendly smile. With a slight wave to the other recruits she acknowledged everyone and sat back down again.

"Recruit Barclay, Sophia."

When she stood up, her personality spoke volumes and demanded attention. She was not tall, not more than five feet three. Her body frame showed that she was used to physical exercise. She looked to be twenty years old, she had short white blond pixie style hair. She turned and looked at each recruit with her emerald green eyes. Just as she was about to sit down, Melissa noticed tattoos of the number nine all up and down her left arm as well as a large enneagram on her left shoulder. Melissa wondered, *She's really into this Watcher thing.*

"Recruit Cosby, Mason."

Nervously, a young sixteen-year-old male recruit stood. He had short straight brown hair, about five feet ten inches tall. His body, muscular for his age, probably played football. Mason was in good shape for his age. He turned and nodded shyly with his dark eyes looking downward before quickly taking his seat.

"Recruit Daniels, Jadon."

This one was older than the other recruits, twenty-five years old, standing at six feet two inches with the body of a runner. He had long legs and wore his long dark brown hair in a braid that hung down his back—braided Native

American fashion. He wore a leather neck piece. He glanced around at the other recruits and took his seat.

"Recruit English, Alexander."

Stretching, this one was a little arrogant, very self-assured. Smiling he looked every recruit in the eye as he said, "Call me Alex." Eighteen years old, around six feet tall with a wiry build. Light brown hair with a bit of curl, hoops in his earlobes. When he reached up to touch his goatee, Melissa could see a small tattoo of the number nine on each of his fingers. His light blue eyes were bright and friendly. With a small wave of his hand he sat back down.

"Recruit Fuller, Melissa."

She stood. Not a spotlight person, she felt like everything faded into the background and she was on display. A bit nervous as she glanced around not really knowing who was new to the family and who was not. Her mouth felt tight as if she were smiling just a bit too brightly. She stood and nodded as she flipped her brown hair back over her shoulder and sat back down.

"Recruit Matthews, Noah."

Noah, twenty-six years old, six feet in height stood up and gave a small wave to the recruits. His hair, thick short strawberry blond hair, and his eyes green. Noah has a slim body and face with a close cut beard and mustache. With a nod to each recruit he sat back down.

"Matthews is now on phase two of his training. I've asked that he assist me with our field training in the next few weeks. I appreciate your assistance."

Noah nodded in answer to her. "Recruit Orange, Amalia."

A young Asian woman, about twenty-one years of age, quietly stood up. She looked to be around five feet tall with long dark brown hair and dark brown eyes. Melissa watched her and thought, *She has a quiet beauty that seem to softly draw everyone in.* Amalia said a soft, quick hello before taking her seat again.

Emma nodded before turning back to the table next and laying her clipboard down. "That's about all on my part. The rest of the evening is yours, so get your personal items in order and stored in your lockers. Guys on the green side, gals on the orange. The next time I see you, you will be on the field in front of the barrack at 0500. For the next thirteen weeks, we'll start each morning with a three mile run, then meet back here for crunches, pull ups, and end with flexed arm hangs."

Walking down the center of the room, Emma eyed each recruit. "Once the physical training is over, hit the showers and be at the mess hall for breakfast no later than 0800. By 0900, breakfast will be completed and you'll need to be at the training facility no later than 0915, standing in right arm formation. By this, I mean each recruit's right hand should be placed on the shoulder of the recruit standing next to him or her, like so…"

Emma stood up and called Matthews to the front to stand with her.

"Matthews, front and center! Now, I'll reach out, touch your shoulder like so. Each recruit will do so each morning during your thirteen weeks of manual training at the center. While at the facility, you will learn to use your energy blade, each of you will receive your solid gold band, and an enneagram tattoo on the right side of your forehead. At the end of your thirteen weeks training you'll receive your official uniforms. At this point, you'll begin the second phase of your training. The second phase will take place at the digital training center called the Digital Cortex of Life, which will prepare you for combat situations. In the meantime, you will train physically and manually with the energy blade while you learn the details of your gifts and the reasons for them. You are now officially in the first stage of phase one. Are there any questions? No? Well, rest assured, before your training is over, you'll have plenty of them! See you tomorrow at 0500."

Melissa walked into the barracks, looking around, watching as each recruit chose their bunk and started placing their personal items and clothes in their lockers.

"Hey, I wonder what's on TV," Alex English said as he walked over and reached for the remote. Within moments, the screen came alive with music and bright colors. Melissa was still in awe of this magical world of technology, it never ceased to amaze her. The screen still flashed bright colors in circles, going in and out, up and down, over and over. Eight pairs of eyes turned to watch, the music stopped and a voice started speaking from out of the mixture of colors.

"Good evening, Watchers. Welcome to Rock Island Training Facilities. During your time here, you will complete two training phases. At the end of these phases, you will then be prepared for a third phase; however, at that time your commander will no longer be your trainer or instructor during your third phase. Nor will the third phase take place on Rock Island. At this point in time, this information will be on a NTK or need- to-know basis only. Your commander will inform you when the time is appropriate. Again, welcome to Rock Island."

"Well, English, I feel better. Thanks for keeping all of us updated and informed, what would we do without you?" Sophia spouted sarcastically as she flopped on the bottom bunk, punched her pillow in place then laid her head back.

"You know, Barclay, that was good info. I didn't know there was gonna be a third phase. Makes sense though, but where do you think that's going to be?" Daniels flipped his braid back over his shoulder as he unpacked his duffle bag while placing all his things in his locker.

"Well…" Barclay mused as she spiked her hair with her fingertips. "I grew up in a Watcher family, I've heard all kinds of stories. I know I had to travel back in time to do my training, so I'm guessing we're going forward to my time—home."

Melissa stood still at the door. She had been looking around the room, but when Sophia said she was from the future…. "Look, y'all, I'm just a simple person. All of this is crazy to me," she said in her slow, southern drawl. She wiped her hand over her face, her eyes were wet. "I'm from the past, I'm from the 1800s. Does that sound insane?"

She looked at everyone's face. They all looked at her as they shook their heads. Daniels closed the drawers of his locker and sat down on his bunk. "Fuller, I wasn't born into a Watcher family and I had no connection at all with the Watchers, but I'd heard of them. I'm from the future. When I was approached by a Watcher and they explained the situation to me, about my gifts, teaching me about the sect of Watchers, I was glad! I easily accepted it, because for the first time in my life, I had a purpose. I understood why I always felt so out of place. Here, well, I fit in, I belong!"

Melissa walked over to an empty bunk and sat down. "Jadon, I'm not like you, that's not how it is with me. I always felt like I belonged, my parents loved me. But I was in the middle of a civil war!" She rolled her eyes. "Anyway, my mother was a Watcher, I just didn't know it. Her name was Tessa. She was the commander's partner before she met my dad. I saw my dad and my mother both murdered, and the next thing I know I'm sitting in a lab being examined by a Dr. Jacob who is a Seeker."

The other Watchers responded with amazement. They had heard of Tessa. This made Melissa feel even more misplaced, these people seemed to know her mother better than she did. The recruits sat on their bunks and exchanged bits and pieces of their lives as they put away their things and clothes and prepared for bed. Melissa was still confused but feeling better knowing that even though these other Watchers were more knowledgeable concerning the ins and outs about the Order of Seekers; at least they, too, were new and just starting their training and had just as many questions. She also felt better because she finally said out loud, what she was afraid of—not understanding her past and not knowing her future.

The next morning, at 0500, the recruits were dressed in their sweats performing their stretches and prepared for their three-mile run. Even though spring had started, the weather was still cool, the fog had settled in and hung low around the lower end of the falls where the water tumbled loudly over and through the rocks. It rushed to meet the deep blue waters of the river surrounding the island. Melissa finished her stretches and started running in place as she focused on the trail leading down through the woods. *What an awesome morning the Creator had given, she thought. I'd rather be doing something else right now.* Then a picture of her mother's face came to mind and all the things she had given up, the gifts she had passed along to Melissa so she could be here today. I've got a responsibility, she thought fiercely. Stay focused, Melissa. Turning, she bumped into Sophia Barclay.

"Hey! What dimension are you in?"

"Oh, sorry." Melissa studied her for a second or two. Today, her short white blond hair was spiked straight up all over her head. She had on a black tank top and stretch pants with a pair of candy spray-painted quilted combat boots.

"So, what's up? You wear glasses, did you forget your con tacts, or what?"

"No, just have a lot on my mind."

Melissa pulled her hair back into a ponytail.

"Well, I like your tank top. I've always been a big fan of the Mouse," she said with a laugh.

Melissa glanced dropped down to her own tank top and black leggings. She had on a pair of hiking boots. Running her hand down over her top, she flushed.

"Yeah, well, it's my favorite. Look, I'd like to stay and chat and all that, Sophia, but I gotta run."

She slipped past Sophia and ran down the trail toward the woods. "Fuller, wait. Mind if I run with you?"

"No. Just don't slow me down."

"Look, if there's going to be any slowing down, it'll be you, not me," she bragged. Melissa felt a tap on the shoulder and a boot kicking into the side of her boot as Melissa ran past her down on to the trail ahead. Catching up to her, they kept a steady pace, until finally coming out into an open field in front of the barracks where three other recruits, Adams, Crosby, and Daniels, were well into their warm ups. The other three, English, Matthews, and Orange, soon came up from behind and joined in on the warm ups. Sweating from an intense workout, Melissa was starved and ready to eat, she headed for the showers.

"Hey, wait up," Sophia said. "Meet you afterward? We'll head for the mess hall together."

With a nod from Melissa, Sophia turned and went off for the showers. Melissa shook her head. *Strange.* She wasn't sure why Sophia picked her to hang out with. *Oh, well, stranger things have happened, I think?*

Now dressed in their temporarily issued uniforms (gray khakis with gray cotton T-shirts) she and Sophia headed down to the mess hall along with the others for a well-earned meal.

"If I keep eating this way, I'll never fit through the barracks' door!"

Sophia looked over at her. "Yeah, well, some of us got it, and some of you don't." Patting her flat stomach, she laughed at the surprised look on Melissa's face and stepped in front of her and started filling up her tray with food.

Melissa rolled her eyes, thinking, *Well, it takes all kinds. I might take her on as a fireteam partner. We'll see, no telling how things might go.*

The mess hall smelled like heaven, each recruit piled on the eggs, bacon, pork sausage links, grits or hash browns, and toast. There was coffee, water, orange juice, and milk. Quickly, the recruits went through the line, sat down, and started eating. Before long the bell went off, trays were emptied and put away as recruits made their way to the training facility. Emma was standing in front of the building with a whistle around her neck and a clipboard in her hand. Each recruit lined up in three rows, three people in each row, facing forward and reaching out with their right hand touching the shoulder of the recruit next to them.

"Ten–hut!"

The recruits came to attention, straightening their shoulders and spines with a stiff snap, their arms by their sides facing forward. Every eye focused on an invisible point just beyond their commander.

"To my right is a table."

Eight pairs of eyes shifted to follow the direction of the commander's words.

"You'll find eight solid gold wrist bands. Inside each band is a recruit's last name and symbol. The history of this energy blade came from the Ancient art of Energy Weaponry. So for the next thirteen weeks your training will be in the Ancient form of Weaponry. The energy blade is a signature weapon wielded by the ancient priests, the strongest and most gifted humans of that order and in the human race; the Seekers, in part, the Watchers. Although, we are human, we've been especially blessed by the Creator with long life and a strong mental capacity, the ability to use 50 percent of our cerebral cortex. The Creator has extended our life span for the special purpose to guard and protect humanity. We are not to abuse or take advantage of these gifts or powers for our own usage or benefit. The energy blade, which the Creator introduced to the first Watcher, Adam, when he gave him the first of its kind, was brought down to earth's atmosphere by one of the Creator's messengers. This blade works in conjunction with the energy and power of the cerebral cortex that flows from the mind through the body of the Watcher into the energy blade to activate and connect to the thick gold band you'll wear around your wrist at all times for the rest of your existence. It will become your way of life. You will not survive as a Watcher without it—your blade will be an extension of you and your personality."

The air was still and filled with quietness as the recruits took in their commander's words. Little by little these young men and women, new Watchers, were becoming conscious of the awesome commitment they were about to make and the heavy responsibility that came along with this. Like the commander had previously said, if they did not have questions at the beginning they would have plenty by the end of their training phases. Melissa could feel the question filling up the spaces in her mind. Which one should she ask first? Which one was most important? If she thought about it too long, she was absolutely sure she would turn and run so far away she would never find her way back again! She slowly became aware of Emma's voice.

"This being a signature weapon, along with the enneagram symbol, means that it is easily identified with the Order of the Watchers. This symbol has been engraved inside your gold band along with your last name. When you first arrived at the training center, you went through a medical examination. During your exam, DNA was taken and applied to the clasp of the band so only you can open, close, or activate your energy blade. In this first phase of your training, this connection and activation will become a natural action you'll do without a second thought. It will become second nature to you. So please remember to take off your band when you sleep at night, at least, during training. I'd hate for you to wake up in the middle of a fight and not know what's going on or how it even started. Believe me, it's happened before! Once you've completed your training, your energy band will be a part of your person, you will not be parted from it. Only during training while you're learning do I ask that you take off your energy bands."

Emma laughed as she turned and glanced down her list of notes then continued her instructions to the recruits.

"Alright, form a line and pick up your gold band. You'll begin your training as soon as you get back in place."

With all the recruits back in line, their gold bands carefully in their hands, Emma watched with interest as each one returned to their position and slid the solid gold band over their hand while tightly closing the clasp shut around their wrist. Suddenly, as if by some silent signal, each young Watcher held up their wrist and stared at the band, feeling the smoothness of the gold with their finger around their wrist. With a slight smile, she stood for a moment in silence before speaking.

"In watching all of you getting acquainted with your band, it brought a memory to mind. I remember the first time I placed my gold band around my wrist. This is an important moment in your memories, one you'll never forget. And I want you to get used to the feel of your band so much so you'll feel naked without it!" she stressed as she pointed to the band clasped around her wrist. "I want it to become a part of you, a part of your persona."

The air around the facility was filled with emotions. Stepping forward, Emma held out her right hand and immediately her blade shot quickly forward from her gold band as a swift shaft of light, emitting a vibrant hum, full of magnetic energy. The blade was extended forward to its full length for all the recruits to see! It was magnificent in all of its electric beauty!

"This is Dothan, meaning faithful. He has not failed me once in battle or at any time I've fought. He and I have been together for years. For many years, my best friend, Tessa, and I fought side by side with our energy blades. Dothan always came in strong for me as Haidee, the modest, did for her. When my friend was killed, her blade vanished, which isn't unusual since energy blades are controlled by the cerebral cortex. When a Watcher dies, and their lifespan on earth ends, the connection to earthly objects is no longer necessary. So ends the need for the energy blade—they vanish." With those words Emma's blade disappeared into her gold band.

"We're going to work on thought and energy flow, teaching yourselves to focus on the energy flowing from your cerebral cortex to the pulse located beneath your gold band. As soon as you get the hang of this, you'll then feel a connection with your blade. Once your connection is made, you will know what your energy blade wants to be called. Don't be surprised by your blade's name. It does not ensure your blade's name will be of your same gender."

Laughing, Emma stopped for a second and pressed her index finger and thumb to the bridge of her nose. Shaking her head, she smiled.

"I remember when I heard my blade's name. Well, at first it scared me because I didn't expect to hear a voice. I guess I thought maybe a whisper? You'll hear your blade speak in its own unique way. Anyway, I ran to Tessa and asked her what her blade's name was, she told me. For about a week I would not speak to my blade. My commander came to me and asked me what was going on. I explained that I had a man's blade; there must have been a mix up. He told me to go and get my blade. I did and we sat down. Then he asked me to call my blade. I said, "No, I can't, it's not mine, it belongs to a man. I think someone has my blade." My commander again asked me to call my blade out. So I slid my gold band on and held out my arm, Dothan immediately came. I told my commander, "My blade's name is a male, what went wrong?" He then explained to me that there was no special meaning or reasoning for this except that the Creator chose to put me with a male energy blade, it's as simple as that, just one of life's mysteries. So it'll be the same with you. The Creator doesn't always work in the way we do, his thoughts are much higher than our thoughts and so are his ways. At all times, he does what will serve best for you. Alright! Secure your bands!"

Emma listened as each recruit again snapped their bands into place around their wrists. She then began to lead them through the steps of energizing their blades. The first day, there were a few sparks from one or two of the recruits, but on the whole, the process of mind over matter was not as easy as it sounded.

"Don't get discouraged and don't stress it. Just go with the flow of your thoughts. Next, I'd like for each of you to go over the test you were given while being flown to the island. This test was given to you so we could learn in which areas you're inclined to be gifted. In the first phase, you'll learn how to use your gifts during field simulations. We will do this manually, so that you can get used to the feel of your blade and get used to activating it while interacting with each other. During all of your training you will find and learn ways to develop tactical and strategic solutions during a battle situation. These war games are used so one can readily discover how one will react in certain given conditions. For example, when you're distracted and your energy blade deactivates, how will your assigned partner respond? Or should the situation be in reverse? There will be other simulations, which will cover a wide range of strategic activities. Within the next week, we will test new ideas, but continue to use the same skills and gifts you already have within you during these simulations to sharpen and hone your abilities to the very best. When we move forward to phase two you will continue your training with the DCL. While all training is completed by holograms in phase two, in phase one you are given a realistic idea of how you will feel when meeting your enemy face to face. In this type of situation, actual combat, your responses will always surprise you because I believe there is nothing that can absolutely prepare any of us for real-life combat."

The recruits' first week of training was exhausting. The stress alone had them quickly seeking out their bunks after mess hall at the end of the day.

Late one evening, at the end of a training exercise, the recruits were dog tired and lined up in the usual right-arm formation. Emma walked over to stand in front of the group. Stopping, she turned and looked over their tired faces and bodies. The exercises with their energy blades had been taxing that day. Even though the names of the blades had been revealed, the techniques were not so easy to master for some.

"Before you hit the showers, I'd like to commend you all on your efforts so far. I know it's hard and you probably feel you have more failures than victories, but don't give up yet. I've heard most of you have gotten to know your blade, consider that a huge accomplishment in itself! Now, the next part of your training will be to learn the responsibility and discipline of being a Watcher."

Looking down at her clipboard she ran her finger over her list. "There's been a change in the daily routine, breakfast we'll meet here at the barracks, split up into two fireteams and go on a training mission. Matthews, you'll take one team while I'll lead the other. Barclay, Fuller, and Daniels will be with Matthews, and the rest of you will go with me. For the next four weeks, we'll be on the less inhabited side of this island. I've found it's the best training grounds for new recruits. There are still a few surprises left, but not anything you can't handle or at least learn how to while you're out there! Oh, another thing, we'll be working on is communication. Not all of us have that ability; you'll understand what I mean by that once we're out there. I'm looking forward to this one! I think you will, too, once you get a taste of what's going on. Okay. hit those showers, not much more to add on here. See ya in the mess hall. Dismissed!"

The following morning, the recruits were up early getting ready for the training mission. Everyone was dressed in black polyester tank tops, tan convertible pants, and gray mountain hiking boots. Emma walked in and out of the young Watchers as they packed their backpacks, checking to make sure that everyone had their supplies packed and ready for the mission.

Melissa turned and looked back over her right shoulder, checking out her over-the-shoulder backpack to see if it fell into place as she secured it around her waist. She had never seen a backpack suspend away from the back like this before. It must be for the air flow for the back area. *Awesome!* After the inspection of backpacks, the two fireteams set out for the mountain trails. Emma was at the front with the first fireteam. She turned to face the Watchers, held up her hand, and said with a raised voice, "We're heading to the west side of the island. In the late 1800s, there was a small town built back in the wooded area. I believe the town was called Douglas Bridge Connection, so you if see signs with this name you'll know we've reached the town. There was a goldmine, so watch your step over there around the mine shaft. You'll see an old trading post, a public library, one or two stores, maybe a bar or two. Sorry, it's a dry state. No drink's been served there in a long time, so no breaks today." She heard moans and groans at her corny excuse for a joke. Yeah, she didn't think it was funny either.

"Okay, okay, I get the point, let's get back to history. At one time, there were a couple of horse stables. Oh! On the land mass on this side of this island is about seventy-six square miles, so you'll be walking through lots of trees, creeks, hills, and such. Great spot to connect with your energy blade and use every chance you get to practice your skills. Don't forget about your gifts and abilities while you're out there. Okay, let's get going. Groups, keep in contact."

All that day, the two groups walked the long trail up along the side of the mountain. The left side dropped straight down about a hundred feet, all rock with a few trees and green ferns here and there. At one point, the group had to pass through a thick growth of oak trees whose branches had grown long and very thick for years. Their roots were now wrapped around the rocky mountain path. Here, nature seemed to have taken over and made a natural bridge about a mile long. Just as the group was coming to the end of the bridge, Alex and Amalia were lagging behind, engrossed in conversation about the history of the island. They were the last to leave the bridge and not really paying attention until someone yelled out, "Snake, snake!" Amalia looked up and saw just above them a light yellowish brown colored snake about twenty-eight inches long, just as it dropped down, falling heavily around Alex's shoulder. Alex stood still, startled, watching the snake's forked tongue whipping in and out in front of his eyes. The other Watchers were motionless, rooted to the spot where they stood, watching to see what Alex was going to do, how he was going to handle this one. Amalia whispered across the moist air, her words echoed through the tree branches that stood around them. Melissa listened as her whispers grew louder until the other Watchers became aware of her words. Melissa was mesmerized as she watched.

"Alex," Amalia whispered. "Be still. That snake hanging around your shoulders…well, it's a golden lancehead."

"Golden lancehead?" he whispered.

"Yes, and it's venomous, so shush, keep ver-r-r-y still, okay? Shh…"

Without a word, Amalia stretched out her hand, her eyes focused on the snake and raised her hand now cupped, and reached out into the air. At the same time, she began to remove the snake from Alex's shoulder as if she were physically holding the snake's head. The force that radiated from Amelia's hand was so intense the golden lancehead looked like a shaft of solid melted gold. She threw the snake with such force and speed, she was brushing her hands together before anyone realized the situation was over.

That night after the fireteam commanders had checked their positions and made camp, everyone sat around eating their rations and thinking over all that had happened that day. Amalia had saved Alex's life. She had used her energy and turned the snake into gold. Emma cleared her throat. She was sitting on an old box next to the campfire while drawing in the dirt with a stick. Watching her stick move in the dirt, she began talking. "I know you were shaken up by what you saw today." She looked up, looking around at everyone. Some were looking down at their golden wrist bands while others watched her.

"I'd say you were even shocked by what you saw," she said with raised eyebrows. "This is just a taste of what you're going to experience during this field mission. It's the reason for the mission—to find and learn your gifts and to find out how to use them during a combat situation. Amalia was probably more surprised by all of this than the rest of you. She acted purely by instinct, her gift is to protect. She is what the Watcher call a 'shield.' Today that was just a snake, but beware there are demonic existences or evil forces out there that come in different forms we call shape-shifters. With training, you'll learn to recognize them before they have time to trick you with their 'glimmer' spells. All I'm saying this evening is to be careful, be aware, and stay watchful. Finish your meals and bed down for the evening. We'll need to be up before the sun."

The next morning, the two fireteams were up and ready before the sun. They walked along the rock-filled path, watching the sun come up while brushing branches and vines out of their faces. The only sound that broke the silence was the bottoms of the boots that hit the rocks and dirt on the path as they headed up the mountain. *The silence would have been peaceful had it not felt so unnatural, so paranormal,* Melissa thought. Just up ahead, the teams came to an old two-story brick building with double doors. Over the doors, a sign was posted, Rock Island Hospital. The architectural structure was phenomenal. The building in its day must have been beautiful. However, now the bars in the windows with dried vines and moss growing in and out of the bars were the only things left. Some of the building's bricks had been knocked out of place leaving large holes in the walls, giving a clear view of what must have been top-of-the-line hospital equipment. There were rusty bed pans, broken gurneys, and beds. Across the room there was one, maybe two, suture tables that had been left behind; only time and age had taken their toll and use of them. About three yards from the building was a group of old birch trees that looked to be about fifty to eighty feet tall. The leaves were light green, yellow, and orange. Melissa looked around to see moss covering the ground and the roots of the trees. Sophia leaned in toward her and said, "Must be a lake or pond close by, those are water birches."

The next building was a small school. One of the classrooms still had books on the small desks. There was writing still partially visible on one of the chalkboards and the bookshelf still had several books stacked in. The walls of the building were now bare of paint, nothing left but memories of what once was. It's sad really, like pictures of someone's life cut short before their time. Some of the rooms had small benches built into the bottom half of the windows. Where had everyone gone to so quickly? It looked as if everyone stopped right in the middle of their workday and just walked away.

Emma called the teams together. "Let's meet at the docks, get instructions, and then split up into teams for individual missions."

Melissa reached for Sophia's top and pull on the back of it. She turned to see what Melissa wanted, raising her eyebrows at her. "What?" she whispered.

"Well, none of this makes sense. What happened, where did all the people go? Why aren't there any people here now?" Sophia shrugged, turned, and walked for the docks. The docks had cement and brick indentions made into them where visitors or workers once hitched their small boats when coming to the island from the mainland.

Melissa couldn't help herself. When she looked at the docks, she felt sorry for this place, it looked lonely, there were no more visitors or residences for that matter. What had happened here?

Emma gave everyone their team instructions and reminded them that Noah Matthews would lead one team while she would lead the other. The teams went their separate ways, Melissa was in Matthews' team. Since it was late, the fireteam found a site and set up camp. "Okay, guys, let's gather in a circle." Everyone met in a circle making plans for the following day. Matthews gave duties to each recruit, and then each ate their day's rations and turned in.

Melissa pushed herself down into her sleeping bag and turned on her side to watch as Sophia did the same. "Sophia, I was wondering, does it feel as if this part of the island has a life of its own? I don't know, I mean… I can almost feel it, don't you?"

Sophia beat her pillow into submission, her usual bedtime ritual. "What do you mean you feel something? I know you have special gifts, Melissa. I mean you're Tessa's daughter after all. Don't give me that look! The only reason I made this team, well, my gift is healing, I'm a healer. I have other gifts, but that's my major gift and the reason I was allowed to make the choice, you know, to become a Watcher."

She turned over, facing Melissa and propped her head up on her hand. "I've had contact with a few Seekers. Well, we need them, they're great record keepers and wonderful researchers," she said with a long drawn-out sigh. "But I wouldn't wanna be one, know what I mean?"

Melissa didn't want to answer that, "Well… getting back to the subject, it's almost like a living organism. My skin can almost feel it breathing, I don't know how to explain it. Maybe I'm tired, I don't know, let's go to sleep. The morning comes way too early around here!" Melissa turned over trying to concentrate.

She felt there was no way she was going to shut down her mind tonight. "Wait... I'll quote the old writings from the Creator: 'Do not let evil defeat you, but defeat evil by doing good. Shalom, I leave you, my shalom I give to you; but not as the earth gives! Do not let your heart be troubled or afraid.'" Just having these words in her heart and mind allowed her mind to slow down and her thoughts to close off. She slowly drifted away into sleep.

Melissa could hear noises slipping through the haze of her sleep, a dull clanging that kept going on and on and on.

"Get up, you lazy good for nothings. It's breakfast on the grill in five. If I don't see your smiling faces then it's all going to these birds that woke me up *early* this morning! Up and Adam!"

Melissa pulled her pillow over her head; the sun wasn't even up! She could hear the rest of them stirring around getting dressed. Matthews started in again, yelling when Daniels, to everyone surprise, bellowed out, "Alright, Dud! Message received!" Within five minutes everyone was eating while pulling their gear together for the day's mission.

"Alright, team, we have a way to go today before we reach our designated stopping point. Let's stick together. I'll chose, at times, for one or two of you to break away and explore and come back with a ground report. We are on this mission to practice our blade exercise and abilities. Let's go!"

The team was back on the old trails again until they reached an enormous grove of Aspen trees, which reached out for about four miles. As Melissa walked through the trees she studied the leaves and watched the breeze as it stirred the leaves on the tree branches. She thought, *It's almost as if the wind is visible when it presses against the leaves, making the tree look as if it's trembling.*

Finally, they came to a clearing. Matthews decided this was a good time for the Watchers to introduce their blades. "This has always been one of my favorites, introduce your blade. I'll go first."

Matthews stepped forward. He held out his left wrist and called out on a whisper the name of his blade, Amit. The energy and power could be felt as Amit, meaning friend, came forward and was introduced as Noah Matthews' partner and energy blade. Then he was gone. Jadon Daniels introduced Isi, which meant deer. Sophia Barclay introduced Loren, which meant "she knows." When it was Melissa's time, she was nervous. She had never been a spot-light personality sort. This made her feel uncomfortable, but she stepped forward anyway. Her first step of faith for the Creator. Her mind was clear and strong every time she thought of her energy blade. She envisioned a bright light. Swiftly, her wrist was warm. She thought, *Enid.* She opened her eyes, and her blade stretched out in front. She was beautiful! Melissa felt blessed that the Creator had gifted her with this beautiful blade. The name of Enid meant 'soul or life.' In place of her mother and father, the Creator had gifted her with a new energy—the very soul and life of her mission. She had a new purpose and meaning in life now. Quickly, Enid vanished back into her golden wrist band.

Close to the end of the day, Matthews sent Melissa out on a mission detail. He gave her three objects to collect and to add to her ground report when she came back. Melissa pulled her backpack over her shoulders once again, looked back at the group, and glanced over at Sophia who was becoming her close friend. Sophia nodded encouragingly at her. She turned her eyes back to the dirt path as she scuffed her booted toe. She walked down a little way before her senses took over and whispered to her. "Look beyond the curtain of trees, just a little way down the road." Being alone for the last hour had played on her mind, now her thoughts went back to Amalia and her new-found ability of shielding. At first she had been afraid, not only because of what had happened, but because of the snake. But the way Amalia had reached out with her hand as if she were actually touching the snake amazed her. She picked it up and got rid of it, she saved Alex's life! I want to be useful like that, *I want the Creator to use me too. I don't want to be afraid anymore,* she determined within herself. Her senses had painted a picture of what had happened. Seeing it again helped her to put it all in perspective.

Melissa pulled aside the branches as if they were made of silk, softly and quickly brushing them away up until she came to a very large old oak tree. Its old limbs were bent and tangled with age but held a beauty that only age and fast held secrets could give. This tree had seen many years and watched many lives, both good and bad. Still it stood there with its branches resting peacefully on the ground and reaching toward the heaven. The tree had been here for so long the roots had started growing above the ground. Melissa stood there in silence. This oak was in its own dimension, a place out of time.

"Melissa…"

She heard a voice calling her. Startled, she turned to the left. Once again. "Melissa…"

Her eyes darted to the right. The masculine voice was friendly yet persuasive. It flowed effortlessly as it spoke to her. She jerked her head around in the direction of the voice. All she could see was the fog spreading across the ground. *How did it get so foggy so fast?* The ground where she stood now looked like a marsh. It was soft and watery and had turned boggy under her feet, the path was now miry and wet. The air appeared heavy as small particles of water vapors formed in the air. Melissa could barely see her hand in front of her face. Squinting her eyes, she searched to find a person to go along with the voice. There, she saw him. He stood just beyond the shadows of the small trees. He didn't seem to be much older than her. His black hair was pulled back at the nape of his neck, exposing his handsome face for her to see. As she studied him, she noticed he was wearing a brown leather vest that showed off his broad shoulders and muscular arms. His long legs were covered with pants made of the same material, and he wore a pair of sandals on his feet.

"Hello, Melissa, I've been waiting to meet you face to face. I've heard so much about you. This is absolutely a pleasure to meet the daughter of one of the greatest Watchers in history."

His smile caught Melissa off guard. Even as the air seemed to clear, she felt his smile was out of place. Looking around, Melissa became aware that she was no longer standing in water, but the marsh had now been replaced with an assortment of beautiful lush flowers of all colors. Even the oak's branches appeared to dance with life. Looking up, she wondered, *Is this another Watcher instructor sent to test me?* She glanced away from the flowers and watched as he glided through the bushes surrounding the garden.

"Melissa, I'm hurt." His white toothy smile flashed across his face, his hand clutched to his chest at his heart as if the very thought or idea of her not knowing him could bring pain. "We've met before. I knew your mother, Tessa. We met in the very same place where you're standing now. It's called Angels Terrestrial, that's the Oak of Angels. It has been here since the beginning of creation, way before this forest came into being. It has provided shelter from storms, provided the moisture and drainage for all the plants that are hidden beneath its branches. So this tree is important to this community, it has been for ages."

Melissa quietly breathed and stood still watching as he continued to approach. She held out her hand. He stopped immediately.

"Don't come any closer. You are close enough for my comfort. I don't mean to be rude, but since I don't know you, that's far enough." She spoke again before he could answer. "Don't give me that argument. I don't want to hear it. Is this part of my training or are you here for another reason?"

"What argument or reason could that be, Melissa? I didn't say anything."

"Yes, you did, I heard your words!"

"No, you heard my thoughts. So...you have your mother's gift. You're telepathic, so am I."

Melissa said nothing—she kept her thoughts to herself. *Oh yeah... well, read this then!*

There was a moment of silence, then Melissa knew he could not read her thoughts. But she kept listening as he spoke, his golden voice hypnotized her, his tone captured her whole attention until she was totally wrapped up in him and fascinated by every word that came out of his mouth. In the back of her mind, she heard another voice screaming at her. The voice sounded familiar. "Melissa...Melissa!" But the pull of this seemingly perfect being's voice was so strong. She pushed the other voice aside.

"You're as beautiful as Tessa, although I sense that your powers, once realized, will be so much more powerful! I think we could work well together. We could do great things together that would give us great recognition. What do you say, Melissa?"

His last words hit her hard! She heard the other voice deep within her, "Melissa...Melissa." She hesitated for a second. "It's me, Emma. Please, listen to me. Yes, you're hearing me. Be careful with your expressions. For now just listen to my words."

She stood there staring forward, confused, a bit foggy-brained, scared, and wondering, *What the heck was going on!? I can hear Emma's voice... in my mind!* She could hear Emma communicating within her thoughts.

"Melissa, you have a powerful gift from the Creator. You're telepathic. You can send and receive thoughts. You are also known as a Discerner. In the old writings, the scriptures, we are told by the men of old who were men of the Creator, 'Do not be shaped by this world; instead,be changed within, then you will be able to decide what the Creator wants for you, if it's good and pleasing to Him,'" Emma quoted to her. She nodded as she kept her eyes on the man in front of her.

"Who are you?"

"My name is Amon."

"You're called Amon?"

Shocked, Emma told Melissa to be very careful as Amon is a dark and dangerous demon from the pit of hell. Taking a deep breath, Emma began to communicate, "I want you to look at the creature, look at the center of his head. Do you see a small slit? Focus on that. Soon, the glimmer spell he's cast on himself will fade, and you'll see him for who he really is."

Melissa focused until she found the slit on the top of his forehead. Slowly his glimmer began to melt away. His beautiful blue eyes turned into a pair of red cat shaped pupils. In a flash, standing before her was a dragon whose scales were bronze. His body was thick with a stubby, slender tail and neck. On the end of its tail was a spike. The dragon's thin limbs had four digits on each foot. It had huge graceful wings that ran from its shoulders to its lower back. Its head was misshaped. Its nostrils were silted. On each side of its head was a strange membrane that function as ears. A bony plate projected from the back of its skull, protecting its upper neck. Two misshaped horns extended straight up from its forehead.

Melissa understood and knew who this creature was and what he had been sent to do. "Amon, the Creator has given you many names. He has also prepared the Watchers in many different ways for when we meet up with you. The Creator taught that while we are under his authority we have the ability to resist you and we have the power to cast you away from our presence so that we don't have to suffer your stench more than necessary. So with the authority that's been given to me, I command that you leave here, now!"

The air reeked of sulfur as Amon howled in pain at the very mention of the name of the Creator, the Ancient of Days! He put his thin arms over his red, cat-like eyes as he dissolved into a puff of black coal smoke, leaving the ground around him burnt and dead.

Melissa stood there, her lungs filled with smoke. Suddenly coughing and gasping for breath, she took in large breaths of air. She had forgotten to breathe while watching Amon dissolve into a cloud of black smoke. She wrapped her arms around her body as she tightly gripped herself in an effort to stop the trembling. Her eyes were staring at the burnt ground that he had left behind. Slowly, she turned and walked back toward camp.

Emma watched as Noah brought his fireteam into the main camp ground. She waited. Melissa looked over at her from across the camp site; the tents, campfires, and the staring eyes of the young Watchers. She was exhausted, drained of all emotion, both physically and mentally. She walked over to Emma and stood in front of her.

"I didn't use my energy blade. I forgot all about it. I don't know if I passed the test or not." Melissa's eyes were filled with tears, but Emma also saw determination, and something the old-timers called backbone. She saw something else in Melissa that she used to see in Tessa, and it was this that led her to believe that everything was going to be all right.

"Melissa, I don't think tonight was a battle of blades, but of will and wit. You learned more tonight than you would've ever learned in a classroom. You have a keen perception of what's going on. With training, your skills and power are going to be on a level with Tessa's. The Creator gifted her with an understanding and intelligence, an astuteness and wisdom, along with a sense of mind like none I've seen before. But Tessa was always a humble person and knew these were gifts from the Creator, nothing she deserved or got on her own. You, too, will need to keep this in mind while you're out there and on your journey in life."

Turning back to the Watchers, she asked them all to gather around.

"Amon, the creature Melissa met up with today is one of the most dangerous evil spirits from hell. He is known as the Grand Marquis of Hell. He is the seventh spirit of the Deceiver himself—Satan! He knows the past and our future, that's because he comes from a place where there is no time. So having this knowledge, for him, is no big deal. It has been said that whoever makes a pact with Satan has to go through Amon first. He comes in all forms. Tonight you saw one of his favorite forms, the dragon!" Emma went on to explain that although he is a powerful demon, the Ancient of Days is the most powerful of all and Amon's powers is nothing in comparison. Turning to Melissa, she said, "Let's meet later. Right now you need to eat, okay?"

Later that evening, as Melissa and Emma sat around the campfire they talked for a while, each taking turns staring into the fire watching the flames fighting its own battle. Emma sat there waiting for Melissa to turn and look at her.

"Melissa, that's not the first time I've met up with Amon. Well, I've not actually had physically contact with him, but Tessa did... twice. The first time, she was about your age, and the second, she was much older. The second time, she knew the battle was going to be fierce. She didn't know that Amon had an ally, a Defector, that's a Watcher who has separated from the Watchers and decided to disobey the code. This Defector was called Elon. He was a powerful Watcher who was at the time a close friend of Tessa's. Elon lured Tessa to a site that he and Amon had preplanned for their attack. As Elon and Tessa sat talking, Amon appeared. Tessa stood up to defend herself. Immediately Elon, who had the power to render a person speechless, took her ability to speak away. Once she realized she couldn't command Amon to leave, Amon attacked her using all his power and forces. He was brutal and held nothing back. Tessa called on Haidee, her blade, and used her other gifts and powers. They battled and raged for hours. Tessa knew she would have to break the spell on her voice, so she struck Amon with a strong blow along the side of his head. The energy from Haidee was powerful that day. He went down dazed and confused. Tessa took that split second and did something that broke her heart, she struck Elon's dead. With Elon gone, the spell was broken, and Tessa was able to call on the authority of the Creator to command Amon to return him to the depths of hell. Tessa was battered and bruised, but, at the same time, triumphant in her victory over Amon!"

Emma went on to explain that Amon had been defeated in many battles many times by powerful Watchers. But that only the Creator of the Universe has the power to destroy him forever.

As she went to sleep that night, Melissa thought about how much her life had changed from that naïve, southern girl into a young Watcher who was now learning to travel through time and fight demons and evil forces. She has yet to learn her gifts, their power, or how to use them. One thing she knew for sure—she would see Amon again, and they would do battle. Until then, she would put her faith and love in the hands of the Great I am, the Creator.